THE BOSS

NICOLA MARSH

Copyright © Nicola Marsh 2023
Published by Parlance Press 2023

All the characters, names, places and incidents in this book have no existence outside the imagination of the author and have no relation whatsoever to anyone bearing the same name or names and are used fictitiously. They're not distantly inspired by any individual known or unknown to the author and all the incidents in the book are pure invention. Any resemblance to actual events, locales, or persons, living or dead, is coincidental.

All rights reserved including the right of reproduction in any form. The text or any part of the publication may not be reproduced or transmitted in any form without the written permission of the publisher.

The author acknowledges the copyrighted or trademarked status and trademark owners of the word marks mentioned in this work of fiction.

First Published by Harlequin Enterprises in 2010 as THE BOSS'S BEDROOM AGENDA
World English Rights Copyright © 2023 Nicola Marsh

Getting up close and personal with the boss...

Beth is the life of the party. She loves shoes, fashion, and her job as a metal sculptor. But when her cousin, the only family she has, needs her help, she swaps her welder for a boring business suit and fills in for Lana as tour guide at the museum. Beth hates everything about the staid job, with one exception. Her gorgeous, grumpy boss.

Aidan 'Voss the Boss' has no time for fun. A archaeologist thrust into the CEO role at the museum, he'll do whatever it takes to make an impression. But Aidan doesn't count on a sassy, brash tour guide upending his well-ordered world. Beth is temptation personified and he's powerless to resist. Opposites attract according to Beth, but he's grumpy to her sunshine and they clash all the time. Except in the bedroom...

Can Aidan lower his guard and take a chance on happiness for once in his rigid life?

CHAPTER ONE

Bethany Walker stuck her tongue out at her reflection as she twirled in front of the mirror. "Do I look geeky enough?"

Her cousin Lana smirked. "I officially pronounce you a bona fide nerd."

Beth turned away from the mirror and glanced over her shoulder to check the back view. "I do look like a nerd, don't I?"

Lana, queen of the nerds and loving it, pushed her tortoiseshell glasses further up her nose as her serious gaze traveled from the tips of Beth's low-heeled black pumps to the top of her strawberry blonde hair pulled back in a tight bun.

"You look exactly how a proper tour guide should." Lana made a dorky tick in the air gesture. "You'll be a great stand-in for me at the museum, no worries."

Beth screwed up her nose as she smoothed the stiff cotton of her ultra plain white blouse. "How could you wear such hideous clothes?"

Lana quirked an eyebrow and picked up Beth's

discarded apple green midriff top and cut-off denim shorts from the floor. "I could ask you the same question."

"Touché, Cuz. Touché." Beth grinned, eternally grateful for the close relationship she shared with her cousin.

From the first moment Lana stood up to her, a mousy six year old that refused to back down when the boisterous, pushy pain in the butt Beth used to be had tried to wrestle a doll out of her hands, their friendship had been cemented.

No-one ever stood up to Beth Walker; not her pushover parents, her preschool friends, or the teachers who doted on the pretty little girl with an off the scale IQ.

How soon that all changed.

"Anything else you want me to cram before I do this? Any last minute pep talk? Instructions? Ways to bore the entire city of Melbourne senseless as they troop through the museum?"

The corners of Lana's mouth twitched. "There is one more thing."

"What?"

She didn't like the gleam in her cousin's eye, the one that screamed she wasn't done turning a swan into an ugly duckling just yet.

"Here." Lana opened the top drawer of her dresser and reached into the back. "You need to wear these to complete the look."

Beth's heart sank as she saw the ugliest pair of glasses she'd ever laid eyes on resting on her cousin's outstretched palm.

Shaking her head, she held up her hands in protest. "Uh-uh. No way. Haven't I done enough? You've dressed me, prepped me, turned me into another you. You can't make me wear those."

Lana laughed. "Relax. I'm kidding. Though I hear these

are the latest fashion statement for all the cool tour guides this year."

"I bet."

Beth rolled her eyes, grimacing at the ugly, black rimmed glasses, ignoring the faintest ring of 'four eyes, four eyes' in her ears.

If she'd hated being a brain as a kid, she'd hated wearing glasses more, and the memories had lasted way too long; until she'd gotten a part-time job at sixteen and earned enough money to buy contacts.

Her dad had no idea why she'd started leaving for school an extra fifteen minutes in the mornings so she could slip into the bathroom to pop her 'eyes' in before the other kids arrived. Not that he would've cared if he did notice.

As for the old saying, 'guys don't make passes at girls who wore glasses' it had been all too true in her case and she'd set about correcting that impression the second those contacts slipped in. She'd transformed from shy geek to flirty femme fatale and hadn't looked back.

Besides, it was easier to be bubbly and have people focused on her extroverted personality than pity her. She may not have had the perfect childhood but pity was the last thing she'd wanted or needed. Only Lana saw through her flirty front and loved her anyway.

"You sure you won't wear the glasses? It would complete your new look." Lana stood back, folded her arms and admired her handiwork, while Beth's ugly shoes pinched and the uglier clothes chafed.

"You're pushing your luck, you know that, right?"

"And you're pushing for time. Time for you to hit the road." Lana tapped her watch as a ripple of pain contorted her face.

"Hey, you need to sit. That ankle isn't going to heal if you don't take it easy. And as much as I appreciate you wangling this job for me for the next few months, you're the one who should be traipsing around that mausoleum, not me."

In all honesty, Beth couldn't be happier Lana had come through for her yet again. She needed this job desperately, and while acting as tour guide at the museum wouldn't set her world on fire, it would take her one step closer to her dream.

"Jeez, you're pushy." Lana slipped crutches under her armpits and hopped to a hard-backed chair a few steps away, before sinking onto it with a barely suppressed groan. "And I will be back on deck just as soon as this damn ankle heals."

She winced as she lifted her leg beneath the knee and propped the ankle on a stool. "Just make sure you do a good job, okay? I don't want you giving the Walker girls a bad reputation before I officially start."

Beth snapped her fingers. "Piece of cake. All I have to do is remember all the stuff you made me cram and take a bunch of curious geeks around the museum. Easy."

Shadows clouded Lana's grey eyes and Beth mentally kicked herself for making light of something so important to her cousin.

"This is my dream job, Beth. I've worked too long and too hard to let this opportunity pass me by just because I was stupid enough to break an ankle." Her expression somber, she plucked at the hem of her top. "The new boss is the son of the old CEO so while Abe Voss hired you I have no idea how tough his son is, and I can't afford anything to go wrong before I've officially started. So just do your best, okay?"

If the sadness in Lana's eyes tugged at Beth's heart, the sheen of tears undid her completely. Her competent, super intelligent, serious older cousin never cried. Lana usually epitomised control while Beth threw tantrums or joked her way into people's good graces, relying on charm and smiles to get through life.

It was easier to smile and hide the pain than dwell on a past she couldn't change.

After giving Lana a swift hug, Beth slid the ugly glasses on and peered over the rims with a mock serious look. "You know I'll do my best. Have I ever let you down before?"

Lana smiled through her tears and rolled her eyes. "Do you really want me to answer that?"

"Actually, no."

They laughed in unison, remembering the countless times Beth had stood her up in favour of a boy, a cool party, or the latest fashion sale.

"Thanks for doing this, Beth. You're the best."

"No, you are," Beth said, wondering if her cousin had any idea how much she owed her and how far she'd go to repay one tenth of the kindness Lana had shown her growing up. Not to mention finding her a job now, when she needed it most.

"Okay, off you go. And remember don't do anything I wouldn't do."

"Yes, boss." She saluted, sending Lana's ankle a pointed look. "Aren't you going to wish me luck? Something along the lines of 'break a leg'?"

Lana pointed at the door. "Out. And take your lousy sense of humor with you."

Beth pouted and stuck a hand on a hip. "Now is that any way to talk to the museum's new amazing tour guide?"

Lana quirked a bushy eyebrow in desperate need of a

good plucking. "Amazing, huh? I'll be happy with good, sensible, dedicated tour guide. You know, the type of tour guide who does a great job and impresses the new boss while standing in for me as I sit back here and get stuck doing lousy paperwork."

"Sensible? Mmm..." Beth grinned, yanked the fake glasses off, placed them in Lana's hand and curled her fingers over them. "Don't worry, Cuz. You can count on me."

She only just heard Lana's murmured, "That's what I'm afraid of," as she strolled out the door, feeling two inches shorter in the awful low heels, missing her staple stilettos already.

"THESE SHOES ARE SOMETHING ELSE," Beth muttered, glancing at the plain black pumps adorning her feet with disdain.

She wouldn't be caught dead wearing shoes like this in public, yet here she was squashed between a sweaty businessman and a scruffy uni student who hadn't discovered the joys of deodorant on a peak hour tram, her feet on display to the world. Not to mention the number of people who would see them as she traipsed through the museum all day.

What she'd give for a pair of sexy sling-backs or a pair of fancy flip-flops right now.

Sighing, she hugged her tote bag tighter to her chest, somewhat comforted by the stab of stilettos through the soft leather. She had a date with an old uni buddy after work and wouldn't have time to head home to change so had brought her outfit with her. The simple knowledge she had a pair of 'real' shoes in her bag made her feel a lot better.

Unfortunately, she didn't feel comforted for long as the tram screeched to a stop outside the museum, she stepped off and took two steps before a low heel caught in the tracks and stuck there. It wouldn't have been a problem if she'd stuck too. However, with a quick glance at her watch sending her scurrying, her body weight pitched forward while the heel didn't and it broke with a resounding snap.

"Justice," she muttered, along with a few unladylike curses Lana would never approve of, as she stared at the ugly heel sticking out of the tracks.

However, her feelings of vindication lasted all of two seconds, as she realized she now had to start work a few minutes late without a pair of shoes.

As if reminding her of their presence, a stiletto dug into her ribs as she tucked her bag under her arm and, making a lightning-quick decision, she grabbed the offending heel out of the tracks, dashed across the road, and sat on a wrought iron bench.

Fishing her favourite stilettos out of the bag, she slipped off the ugly pumps and wriggled her fuchsia painted toes into the sandals, sighing in relief at the luxurious feel of designer shoes adorning her feet once again.

Pushing aside the thought that sexy black patent sandals with tiny straps and adorned with feathers weren't appropriate tour guide footwear, she strode toward the museum as fast as her three inch stilettos could carry her.

With the correct footwear, a girl could face anything and right then, Beth knew her day was looking up.

Those shoes are something else, Aidan Voss thought, as he caught sight of the new tour guide strutting across the polished marble floor toward him, her nose ten feet in the air.

She looked like she didn't have a care in the world rather than a woman who was five minutes late for her first day on the job.

"Miss Walker?"

"Yes?"

If her shoes were something else, her dazzling green eyes captured his attention and shot his interest into the stratosphere. They sparkled with intelligence and even a hint of wariness couldn't hide the glint of fun in their moss-green depths.

"You're late," he said, his gaze roaming over her heart-shaped face with the high cheekbones, pert nose, and lush mouth a tad on the full side.

Her features should've clashed. Instead, they melded into a heart-stopping combination and for a guy who appreciated beautiful things on a daily basis, and had since he could first walk and talk, he couldn't tear his gaze away.

"And you are?"

Surprised by her cocky comeback when she should've been on the back foot, and more than a little annoyed at his urge to laugh, he said, "Someone who could have your butt for waltzing in here late on your first day."

If her confidence surprised him, her glossed lips curving into a saucy smile shocked the hell out of him.

"You could have my butt, huh? Sounds like an interesting way to foster employee relations."

His mouth twitched despite the urge to send this woman packing before she'd begun. From what his father had said he'd expected a mouse-like woman. Instead, apart from her sun-streaked blonde hair pulled back in a tight bun and a drab black suit, this woman screamed sexy rather than tour guide.

Sexy? Where had that come from?

Lowering his gaze to her feet and those funky shoes, he knew exactly what had put the idea into his head. He was a leg man through and through, and the sight of her curvy stockingless calves and dainty feet thrust into shoes belonging on a stripper rather than a conservative tour guide had his head in a spin.

He chose to ignore her sassy remark, considering his obsession with her legs didn't need the added burden of thinking about her butt too.

"I'm not an employee." He mustered his best glower, the one that made most employees jump to his attention on various digs around the world.

Her eyes lit up, sparking green fire as she tilted her chin up. "In that case, you have no right bailing me up. So if you don't mind—"

"I'm your *employer*."

He expected to see fear or the glimmer of an apology replacing the sassy spark in her eyes. Once again, she proved him wrong.

"Pleased to meet you. Beth Walker, tour guide extraordinaire at your service." She stuck out her hand, her wide grin irresistible, and he found himself unwittingly returning her smile while he shook her hand.

"Aidan Voss, the new boss around here."

A boss who had no right noticing how her eyes twinkled when she smiled or the cheeky lilt in her voice when she spoke, as if challenging him to do goodness knows what.

"Do you personally greet all your employees?"

"Only the ones who are late on their first day." He sent a pointed glare at his watch. "I must say your lack of punctuality surprises me, Miss Walker."

"Call me Beth." She dropped her gaze, but not before he'd seen a flicker of fear, the first sign she was anything other than confident. "And I'm really sorry for being late. I was running on time until I had a shoe crisis."

Once again, his lips gave a decided twitch and he clamped down his urge to laugh out loud. "Speaking of your shoes, do you think they're appropriate for your role here?"

She gripped her bag tighter, her knuckles standing out, as he glimpsed another sign Beth 'fancy feet' Walker might be more rattled than she let on.

"Shoes this good are always appropriate..." she trailed off as he frowned at her and her fingers flexed around the strap of her leather carry-all again. "Considering I broke a heel on my pumps in the tram tracks out the front a few minutes ago, I had no choice. It's my stilettos or go barefoot and I'd hazard a guess you wouldn't go for the bare look?"

Finding his gaze drawn unwittingly to those sexy shoes again, he wrenched it upward with effort, determinedly ignoring how great she'd probably look padding around these hallowed halls barefoot.

Clearing his throat, he said, "Just make sure you wear something more appropriate tomorrow."

Her lips curved in a tentative smile. "So that means I'm not in trouble for being five minutes late?"

"Don't push your luck," he muttered, intrigued by the contrasting combination of confident woman one moment, vulnerable new employee the next.

Even now, while her fidgeting fingers on her bag strap

belied her nerves, she met his gaze without the slightest hint of intimidation.

He'd never met anyone like her. Most of the people he worked with deferred to his experience or were in awe of his connections in the archaeological world. As a new employee, she would know about his family and their role in the museum, yet she acted as if he were an acquaintance. Or worse, as if he were a guy she could flirt with.

"If there's nothing else, I'll get started?"

Nodding, he tried another frown for good measure. It had little affect as her sunny smile banished the last hint of any susceptibility and transformed her into cheeky ingénue in a heartbeat.

"Fine. I take it you had a tour following the interview so you know your way around?"

"Uh-huh."

"Then you can start in the Australiana gallery today. It should be quiet in there as we're not expecting many school groups, and Monday's are notoriously mundane around here anyway. Any questions?"

"No thanks. I'm ready and raring to go."

Aidan blinked, struck by how every word tumbling out of her lush mouth sounded like a naughty invitation.

Annoyed at his wayward thoughts, especially in relation to an employee, and hating how she had him on the back foot since he first laid eyes on her, he injected the right amount of coolness into his voice. "That's all for now. Good luck."

Her confident smile never wavered. "Thanks, but I don't need it. I'm good at what I do."

With that, she turned on those ridiculous three inch heels and strutted away—in the wrong direction.

"Beth, the Australiana gallery is that way."

She stiffened and paused mid-step, swinging back to face him and he pointed over his shoulder.

Something akin to panic flickered in her eyes for a second, though it could've been a trick of the light as the bright sun's rays of a Melbourne spring morning filtered through the towering glass comprising the museum's shell.

"I knew that." She fidgeted with the strap on her bag, sending him a tight smile at total odds with her previous self assurance. "I was hoping for a quick caffeine fix before I started."

"The staff cafeteria is that way too."

He grinned, somewhat satisfied to see her flustered as she gripped her bag tighter and swung her head as if expecting to flick her hair over her shoulder.

With a dismissive shrug, she set off in the opposite direction. "I've always had a lousy sense of direction."

"Well, I expect you to get up to speed pretty quick around here. After all, how do you expect to take tours if you need a map and a compass yourself?"

"I'll be fine." Some of her earlier spark returned as she tilted her chin in the air and shot him a haughty glare. "Thanks for the welcome but it's time I started my new job."

He couldn't help but smile at her confidence, eager to return to his office and check out her CV. Either his father was losing his touch at reading people or there was a lot more to their newest tour guide than met the eye.

"I better get started pronto because hear the boss is a compulsive clock-watcher."

With that parting comment, she sashayed away, looking way too appealing for a woman in a boxy black suit, leaving him with an unimpeded view of those sensational legs.

Oh yeah, he definitely needed to read up on his newest employee.

Anyone who could wear shoes like that on her first day and not be intimidated by him was worth watching and he had every intention of keeping a close eye on her.

Very close.

CHAPTER TWO

"Could this place be any bigger?" Beth muttered under her breath, scanning the endless corridor for a sign of the Australiana gallery.

She'd walked the length and breadth of the maze of corridors following clearly marked signs, but had somehow ended up in the dinosaur room, the creepy crawly room, and the reptile room, without a glimmer of Aussie stuff in sight.

"Can I help you?"

Beth inwardly groaned. Just what she needed, someone else chastising her for being late; or worse, lost when she should know her way around.

Fixing a smile on her face, she turned toward the tentative voice. "Actually, you can help me. This is my first day on the job and I was a bit frazzled after the interview when I got the grand tour and can't seem to find the Australiana gallery."

The young woman's bemused expression spoke volumes. She obviously thought the new tour guide was a brainless bimbo.

"I'm heading that way myself."

"Great." She fell into step with the woman whose name badge had 'Dorothy' typed in bold, black print, as she surreptitiously checked out Dorothy's footwear for signs of sparkly red shoes - and not surprised when she found staid black flats instead. "I'm Beth, by the way."

"Dorothy. I'm a volunteer."

"You don't get paid to be here?"

Jeez, she could think of any place she'd rather be if she wasn't doing this for the stability factor. Stable job plus adequate funds equaled a lease on a small gallery to showcase her work and right now, she needed that lease. She'd waited long enough to set her plan in motion.

Not to mention paying off a small fraction of the emotional debt she owed Lana.

"I'm an archaeology student. I do this for a bit of extra experience." Dorothy's brown eyes lit up for a moment, brightening her make-up-less face.

"You must really love what you do."

Dorothy nodded, her bobbing head setting her bun wobbling precariously atop her head.

What was it about buns in this place, Beth thought, wishing she could tug the pins out of hers and shake her hair loose, letting it tumble around her shoulders in a wild mess like she usually wore it.

"And the opportunity to work alongside someone of Aidan Voss's calibre was too good to pass up," Dorothy said.

Beth's ears pricked up. She'd been so busy trying to find her way around this maze that she'd deliberately pushed aside thoughts of her boss.

Guys who looked like Aidan Voss didn't enter her sphere too often. The proverbial tall, dark and handsome seemed way too trite when describing his almost perfect looks. If it hadn't been for the inch-long scar near his right eyebrow, he could've modeled rather than dig around old ruins and keep watch for recalcitrant tour guides.

"So he's good?" Beth kept her tone casual despite the sudden urge to learn more about the guy with the sharp cheekbones, strong jaw, slate grey eyes, and hint of a dimple. Not that she'd memorized every detail of that striking face or anything.

Dorothy's incredulous expression had Beth biting the inside of her cheek to prevent laughing out loud.

"Good? He's the best. Not only does he come from one of the most renowned historian families in Australia, he's been responsible for several major finds around the world. Egypt, South America, Greece, you name it, he's done it."

A faint blush stained Dorothy's pale cheeks and Beth had a feeling the boss's good looks hadn't gone completely unnoticed by the enthusiastic volunteer.

"But surely you know all this? I would've thought the lure of working with a man like Mr. Voss would be irresistible to anyone interested in this business?"

"Oh, working with Mr. Voss is irresistible all right."

Beth's memory worked its way down from that memorable face to the way he'd filled out his charcoal suit, how his pale blue business shirt had stretched across his chest and how he'd strutted rather than walked. In those few minutes he'd bailed her up for being tardy she'd had the impression of a self-assured guy, a guy on top of his game, a guy who could turn a girl's head without trying.

Not that he was her type. She preferred her men scruffier, less domineering, more casual, and the super confident Aidan Voss definitely didn't fit that bill.

Not that she should even consider him as any 'type'. Lana would keel over and break her other ankle if she thought for one second she was sizing up their boss as sexy guy material.

"Well, here we are."

"Thanks," Beth said, momentarily distracted by her thoughts of Aidan as sexy and pulling up just in time to stop slamming into Dorothy's ramrod straight back.

"I'll be fine from here," she added, eager to get rid of the volunteer so she could start doing some serious exploring and familiarize herself with the room. Though she'd studied up on the museum and done some serious swotting with Lana, she couldn't afford to make any more gaffs or draw further attention to herself.

Her job depended on it and in turn, Lana's. She wouldn't mess this up for her cousin. She owed her, big time, and not just for the job.

Dorothy hesitated, toying with her name badge while a small frown creased her brow. "Can I ask you something?"

"Sure." Beth hoped it wasn't a question about the brontosaurus location or where the authentic movie set from an iconic Aussie movie was.

"Where did you get those amazing shoes?"

Beth laughed and wriggled her toes, wondering if it was a meaningful twist of fate that her heel on Lana's drab shoes had broken on her way in.

"I'm hopeless with fashion and I'd kill to have a pair like that," Dorothy added, her tone wistful.

Beth enjoyed meeting new people and making friends; she enjoyed talking fashion more, so she said, "Why don't we meet for lunch and I'll let you know where all the best shoe shops in Melbourne are located?"

"Great. See you in the cafeteria at one."

Dorothy's genuine smile was the first hint of real warmth Beth had seen and as she watched her walk away in her brown pants and matching jacket, with a prim cream blouse, severe hairstyle and not an ounce of style, Beth definitely felt like a makeover could be in order if Dorothy was up for it.

However, when she entered the Australiana gallery and took in the vast array of various displays, she realized she'd made a mistake. She should be focusing on getting up to scratch in here, not indulging her passion for retail therapy. This job was too important and she'd already made a less than favourable impression with her tardiness.

Sighing, she shook her head and headed for the first display. This business of being a *good, sensible, dedicated* tour guide as she'd promised was going to be a lot harder than she thought.

∼

AIDAN SAT BACK in his large leather chair and stared out the wide window at the Royal Exhibition Building framed by a cloudless blue sky.

He loved the old building, had loved this view the first moment he'd entered his dad's office as a cocky archaeological student determined to take on the world. Or more correctly, travel the world in search of the ancient relics that made his pulse pound with excitement and always had since he'd accompanied his parents on his first dig as an inquisitive five year old.

He'd never forgotten the feel of hot sand beneath his hands as he dug alongside them with a miniature spade, the heat of an unforgiving Egyptian sun beating down as he scrabbled harder and harder until he'd found the small mummy figurine his father had assured him was there.

It wasn't until years later he'd realized his dad had

planted it there for him to find in typical puppet-master fashion but by then it had been too late. He'd chosen his path. He'd wanted to be an archaeologist, the best in the business. His dad may have chosen a desk job despite being the premier historian in Australia but Aidan had wanted more, craved more.

Ironic, considering he now sat in his dad's vacated chair, the last place he wanted to be given a choice.

He picked up his cell and tapped the first name in his favourites list, knowing his dad would berate him for interrupting his siesta, remembering times gone by when the indefatigable Abe Voss would've been out and about at this time of the morning, prime exploratory time before the scorching outback sun sent even the hardiest explorer scurrying for shade.

"Aidan. Good morning."

"Hey, Dad."

"What's up?"

Aidan stiffened, Abe's gruff, brisk tone the same abrasive way he'd spoken to him all his life, as if he were an interruption to be tolerated. No niceties, no normal exchange of pleasantries. But then, what did he expect, for his father to change just because he was doing the old man a favor?

Swallowing his annoyance, Aidan swiveled his chair away from the view and picked up Beth Walker's CV.

"I met the new tour guide this morning. She's not what I expected."

"She's something else, isn't she? I knew she'd be perfect for the job."

Something else was right. The minute he'd laid eyes on Beth Walker he'd known she was perfect—though inappropriately, work had been the furthest thing from his mind.

Frowning, he tapped her CV against the desk. "Her credentials aren't super impressive. Tour guide during racing carnivals and at a car show isn't exactly the same as conducting tours here, is it?"

"Are you questioning my judgment?"

Hell yeah. But he wouldn't push it. The only reason he was sitting in this chair was because his father had asked him to. Abe had made the first overture in his life to acknowledge his son's skills and Aidan wasn't about to sabotage the tentative professional mate-ship they'd developed lately.

"I guess her demeanor threw me a little."

"Why? Because she's a tad on the exuberant side?" Abe snorted, an exasperated sound that told Aidan exactly what his father thought of this phone call. "Look, Lana Walker will be a huge credit to the museum. She's the best curator on the eastern seaboard and I trusted her judgment when she recommended her cousin to take tours while she recuperates. Then I interviewed Beth and she's exactly the type of employee we need. Fresh, vibrant, willing to learn. So what's the problem?"

"No problem."

Not unless he counted the awful sinking feeling he was attracted to her when he shouldn't be. CEOs shouldn't fraternise with staff, even ones with sparkling eyes, cheeky smiles, and come-get-me shoes.

"Right, well, if that's all, I have to go. Your mother has me on this crazy exercise regimen."

Aidan paused, knowing Abe hated talking about his health, well aware he'd irritated the old man enough for one day with his interrogation about Beth. "How's the heart?"

"Fine. Blood pressure's down. No angina since we came up here."

"Great—"

"Must go. I'll call you next week to check up on how the place is doing."

The dial tone hummed in Aidan's ear before he'd had a chance to say goodbye and Aidan slid his cell into his pocket, the familiar disappointment clawing at him.

The old man would never change and he'd be a fool to hope otherwise.

Aidan had been shocked when Abe had turned to him for help after doctors advised him to rest or risk a heart attack and his parents made the decision to head for the tropics of northern Queensland.

Aidan hadn't been able to refuse, buoyed by the uncharacteristic action of a man who barely acknowledged his achievements—or existence-growing up, a small part of him still hoping for the unthinkable to happen, that dear old dad would finally recognize his worth.

So here he was, trying to prove a point, aiming to be the best damn CEO the museum had ever seen.

And good CEOs always kept a close eye on employees... Scanning Beth's CV again, he shook his head. Gut instinct had served him well in the past, giving him a feel for the best sites to search, directing him where to dig.

Maybe in this case his instincts were wrong?

However, the more he read of Beth's CV and her apparent lack of skills, and compared it with the mental image he had of the bold, smart-mouthed tour guide, the more he had the feeling she wasn't the right person for the job.

But he believed in giving people a chance so that's exactly what he'd do. However, if the cutesy tour guide made one too many mistakes...he shoved her CV back into a folder and stood up.

He wanted this place running perfectly and the only way to ensure that was to do spot checks on his staff.

Starting with one highly unusual tour guide.

CHAPTER
THREE

"How did it go?"

Beth took a long, drawn out sip of her mocha mint iced chocolate and smacked her lips, trying to hide a grin at Lana's anxious expression and failing.

"This isn't funny, Beth. I'm in agony over here and I'm not just talking about my ankle."

"Okay, okay, hang onto your crutches." She drained the rest of her favorite drink, placed the take-out cup on the coffee table, and stretched. "There isn't much to tell. My first day was uneventful and glitch-free."

Well, almost, if she didn't count her run-in with the way too sexy Aidan Voss first thing in the morning and the slight mishap with the train display later.

Lana frowned, her dubious expression the same one Beth had seen many times over the years, since they'd been playmates fighting over crayons or dolls. "Right. Now tell me the truth. All of it."

Beth blew her cousin a raspberry.

"Where do you want me to start? The part where I

broke my heel on the way in and was bailed up by the boss? Or the part where I got lost traipsing around that monstrosity? Or the part where I befriended this lovely volunteer in desperate need of a fashion makeover and took her shopping?"

Lana's loud groan had nothing to do with her ankle. "Tell me I still have a job."

"You still have a job," Beth replied, parrot-fashion. "As for your credibility as a curator, that's highly debatable."

Lana smacked her head. "Tell me why I let you convince me you needed this job. And why I put in a good word for you. At my place of employment. Where I've finally secured my dream job."

Beth blew her a kiss. "Because you love me. Because this affects my dream too. Because you know I can do it."

And she would, despite the few hiccups on her first day. Besides, it hadn't been too bad and surely everyone went through teething problems with a new job?

Lana sighed and sank back against the cushions propping her up on the couch. "I know, I know, but I'm having a coronary over here, worrying about what's going on over at the museum." She slapped her injured leg and grimaced. "I hate being this helpless and dependent on other people."

"You mean me?"

Lana had an independent streak a mile long. Guess it came with the territory of losing both parents early. In a way, her cousin's tragedy had bonded them in a way nothing else could've. Considering Beth had lost her mom in the same car accident, the two of them had clung to each other, a pair of devastated six year olds with their worlds turned upside down. And hers had never righted.

"I know you're doing your best." Lana's grim expression implied her best wasn't good enough. "It's just that I don't think I can last three months sitting around here doing nothing but paperwork."

"You don't exactly have a choice."

A bit like herself, actually. She owed Lana, and if her cousin had asked her to walk on water she would've. Doing the physical side of Lana's job for a few months was small payback for everything her cousin had done for her. Not to mention the added bonus that she really needed this job.

Her muse had gone AWOL along with her latest boyfriend, taking her chance of having a display in his gallery along with him. Though she should be grateful. The rat's actions had prompted her to finally follow her dream and lease her own space. If the powers that be at the stuffy bank ever let her sign the paperwork, that is.

"Good point. So tell me about the boss. What's Abe Voss's son like? I've heard on the grapevine he's a gun."

Son of a gun, more like it, Beth thought, remembering those slate grey eyes and their calculating expression as they sized her up.

"He's quite impressive."

An unexpected quiver of excitement skittered down her spine as she contemplated exactly how impressive Aidan Voss was.

"His credentials, you mean?"

"I mean the whole package."

Oops. Beth mentally slapped herself for putting together 'impressive' and 'package' in her imaginative mind.

A furrow appeared on her cousin's brow. "I don't like that gleam in your eye."

"What gleam?"

Beth tried her best innocent look and knew it came up lacking when Lana groaned and shook her head.

"The gleam you get whenever any male under thirty-five and halfway good looking enters your sphere."

Tilting her nose in the air like she didn't give a damn, Beth said, "I have no idea of his age. From how tense he appears, he's probably ancient."

"And the good-looking part?"

Trust Lana not to back down. Damn it, she was like a dog with the proverbial bone. Or in this case, the curator with a dinosaur bone.

"He's not bad for an uptight older dude who likes fossicking for boring old artefacts."

Lana laughed for the first time since she'd arrived at her cousin's quaint single story weatherboard in one of Carlton's quieter streets.

"I'm onto you." Lana's laugh grew to belly-shaking proportions. "Your version of not bad equates with sex god. He's that good?"

Beth nodded, joining in the laughter. "Better. Honestly, you should see this guy. Tall, great bod, killer smile, fabulous eyes. A knockout."

"Don't forget the brain behind the *package*." Lana's not-so-subtle emphasis on the last word had them in fits of laughter.

"You'll see him soon enough."

"If you don't get me fired, that is."

Her cousin's laughter petered out as her worried expression returned. Considering the mess Beth had made of her first day on the job, she didn't blame her.

So she did the only thing possible, the one thing she'd done her whole life to cope when faced with uncomfortable circumstances: made light of the situation.

"And deprive you of seeing Voss the Boss in the flesh? Not likely."

Lana cringed. "You know you just called one of the most influential men in archaeological circles Voss the Boss? Just make sure that little gem stays between us."

"You got it." Beth leaned forward, tapped the side of her nose, and lowered her voice to a conspiratorial whisper. "Now, would you like me to bat my eyelashes at him to get on his good side? You know, to keep the Walker girls in favor with the boss."

"Don't you dare."

Lana's eyes widened in horror behind her tortoise-shell glasses and Beth chuckled.

"Don't worry, Cuz. I have no intention of flirting with the boss."

However, Beth had to resist the urge to squirm under her cousin's speculative glance as she quickly pushed aside the thought she already had.

BETH IGNORED the wolf-whistle of a restaurant spruiker as she strolled down Lygon Street on her way to meet Bobby, her date for the evening.

Not that catching up for a drink with Bobby was a date exactly. In fact, the thought of seeing the lanky, red-headed drummer as anything other than friend material brought a smile to her face.

So she'd dressed up? No big deal. She needed to slip into her favorite black mini and shimmery aubergine top to feel half-way normal again after spending all day in an awful suit. She loved her cousin to death but boy, could Lana do with a wardrobe revamp. Though she should be grateful; at least she hadn't needed to buy an entire new nerdy tour guide wardrobe.

As she passed her favorite gelateria and studiously avoided looking in the window to stop from drooling all over her top, her cell rang and she scrambled in her bag, hoping Bobby wasn't standing her up. She needed a drink, some light-hearted conversation, and the inevitable laughs that spending an evening with a fun friend entailed.

It had been way too long since she'd had a good night out; her, the party girl of Melbourne, had spent too many evenings lately holed up at Lana's place, swotting up on the museum. Boring. Time to live a little, just like she used to.

Staring at the caller ID and not recognizing the number, she tapped the answer button. "Beth Walker."

"Hello, Beth. Aidan Voss here."

She stumbled and would've sprawled onto the nearest café table if a kind waiter with the sexiest chocolate brown eyes she'd ever seen hadn't reached out to steady her.

Mouthing 'thanks' at the waiter, whose wink had her beaming back at him, she continued walking while furiously trying to think up something fabulously witty to say, anything other than 'what do you want?'

"Sorry to call after hours but I need to see you."

Uh-oh. Some first impression she must've made.

"I can come in early first thing tomorrow," she said, trying to keep her tone business-like.

"I need to see you now."

"Oh." Damn, that one tiny syllable came out on a sigh and she quickly reassembled her wits. "Sorry, no can do. I have other plans."

"This isn't a request, it's an order."

His silky smooth voice did little to disguise the thread of steel beneath. Aidan was a guy used to making people jump, people who probably asked how high.

"I'm meeting someone," she blurted, gnawing at her

bottom lip the instant the words left her mouth, realizing how stupid it sounded as an excuse. As if high and mighty Aidan Voss would care if she had a date.

"Far be it from me to disrupt your love life but this is important and it can't wait until morning."

"Bobby's just an old friend," she said, refraining from slapping her head, just, as another corker popped out of her mouth without thinking.

Damn it, what was it about this guy that rattled her so much? She usually handled guys with finesse, flirting with them while keeping them at arms length, using quips and witty repartee rather than blurting the first thing that came into her head.

"I'm glad."

He paused and for one, insane second she hoped he might be glad she wasn't on a real date, before realising why the heck would he care. She was an employee, a lousy one at that if his unimpressed tone and his order to see her immediately was any indication.

"That means you can take a rain check and Bobby won't be disappointed. I'll meet you in the museum foyer in an hour."

If this was just about her she'd tell him where he could stick his presumptuous after-hours order, but considering she had to consider Lana's reputation she had no option but to do what he wanted.

"Fine. I'll be there. Though the least you can do is tell me what this is about."

"That incident with the train display today? The child's mother has lodged an incident report and we need to discuss it."

Incident report? Great, just freaking great. As a first day on the job, this one sucked, big time.

Clamping down on the flicker of fear that this pending meeting couldn't be good for her job security—and in turn, Lana's—she muttered her best contrite tone. "No problems. See you in an hour."

"One other thing."

"What is it?"

"Don't be late."

He hung up before she could respond and with a resigned sigh, she flung her cell into her bag.

If it weren't for Lana—and Beth's dream gallery at stake—she would walk away from this less-than-appealing situation and never look back. She wasn't a tour guide, she was an artist, and having to follow someone else's rules didn't sit well with her. She was used to creative freedom, to being her own boss, not jumping to someone else's tune.

As she passed a bright, airy shopfront filled with exquisite paintings and sculptures, she sucked in a deep breath and squared her shoulders.

She wanted that. Her very own space filled with her work, with the autonomy to do what she wanted when she wanted. Recognition for her talents, recognition of any sort if she were completely honest, something she'd craved from her dad and never got.

Casting one last longing glance at the mini-gallery, she tucked her bag tighter and picked up the pace.

She could do this.

She had a job to do and she'd better do it well.

Achieving her dream depended on it.

AIDAN PACED the empty entrance hall of the museum and wondered what the hell he was doing.

He'd had a bad day, starting with a pile of boring financial reports and ending in a complaint from an irate mother.

Though officially his day hadn't been all bad, and it hadn't exactly started off with those reports considering he'd bailed up the new tour guide first thing.

Ironically, he'd be ending his day the same way he'd started: glancing at his watch and shaking his head at Beth Walker's lack of punctuality.

He shouldn't even be here. Confronting her over the train display drama could've waited until morning but something had prompted him to call and order her back tonight.

He muttered a curse, knowing exactly what that 'something' was: fascination.

She had him wound up and he needed to see her now for no other reason than to reassure himself that his absorption with her when he should've been focussing on those reports had stemmed from interest in the skills of a new employee and not an underlying fatalistic attraction he couldn't act upon.

As if on cue, a loud tapping sounded on the glass door in front of him and he flicked the lock, sliding a finger between his collar and neck while doing so.

He needed some air, fast. His lungs had seized the second he laid eyes on Beth, dressed in a shimmery purple top, full make-up, blonde hair sleek, and a black mini skirt that would keep him up all night. Correction, the memory of her long, tanned legs on full display in that micro skirt would do that.

"Let me guess. You're going to tell me off for being a few minutes late." The full mega-wattage of her smile hit him as she flicked her hair over her shoulder in a gesture suggesting habit rather than an attempt to capture his attention.

Not that she needed to do anything other than stand there to do that.

"I saw you staring at your watch just before I knocked," she added for clarification.

"Occupational habit." He ushered her in and locked the door, trying not to inhale too deeply at the tempting fruity fragrance in her wake. "I like things running to clockwork. It's the way I've always worked."

"I never would've guessed."

Her eyes twinkled with amusement as her glossed lips curved into a dazzling smile that slammed into him with the force of a tumbling pyramid.

"Come on, let's go. We have business to discuss."

She didn't bat an eyelid at his gruffness. "So you said on the phone."

Her smile faded and irrationally, he was disappointed.

"Let's wait until we reach my office so you can read the complaint for yourself."

He found his gaze unwittingly drawn to her shoes as she fell into step beside him. The frivolous, fancy, feather shoes with barely there straps completed this outfit much better than the boring suit she'd worn earlier that day and *sexy* instantly sprung to mind again.

Damn it, he shouldn't be thinking this way, shouldn't be noticing things like sexy shoes or her alluring outfit or the way the shimmery silver on her eyelids highlighted the vivid jade depths beneath.

"You don't fit the image of the average tour guide."

She chuckled, her soft laughter as enticing as the rest of her. "So what does an average tour guide look like?"

"Not you," he muttered, glad they'd reached his office.

Most of the lights had been turned off at closing time and walking along the narrow corridor hip to hip with her had him wishing he hadn't suggested this after hours meeting.

Proving to himself he wasn't interested in her was great in theory. Pity the practice did little more than show him up for fraud.

He was her boss.

Which meant she was a no-go zone.

Now he just had to remember it.

Eager to get this over and done with, he flung open the door and gestured her to enter before him. Bad move. If that itty-bitty skirt highlighted her incredible legs, it did amazing things to her butt.

"Okay, let me have it."

He wrenched his gaze up to meet hers in record time but the knowing smile curving her glossed lips spoke volumes: she'd caught him checking her out and was enjoying every minute of it.

Irritated by his slip up, he strode to his desk and handed her the written complaint. "Here. Read this, then we'll discuss it."

She speed read it, anxiously gnawing at her bottom lip while he tried to ignore the crazy urge to do the same. When she reached the end, she ran a shaky hand through her hair, inadvertently draping it over a delectably bare shoulder where her top had dipped.

"So what do you want to do about this problem?"

Furious he couldn't keep his mind on the task at hand and off trifling observations like the subtle glimmer of bronze dusted on that bare shoulder, he gestured for her to have a seat while he perched on the edge of the desk.

"This problem is indicative of a larger one. Namely, you."

Her eyes flashed emerald fire while her bottom lip wobbled slightly. "I wasn't a problem when your father hired me. He thinks I'll be an asset to the museum."

"And do you feel the same way?"

"Of course."

While that tremulous bottom lip suggested she was quaking inside, she eyeballed him, challenge in the green depths, taunting him to break the deadlock and look away first.

Like hell he would.

"My father may have hired you but that doesn't mean I can't fire you."

He dropped the magic F word and she lowered her gaze in record time. Looked like Miss Fancy Feet valued her job more than she let on.

"The train thing was a misunderstanding." She handed him the complaint form and sighed. "It wasn't my fault the little monster was fiddling with the display."

How did she do that, undermine his annoyance with a hint of a smile and a blunt response?

Nothing was remotely funny about this situation—the written complaint highlighted a day filled with her incompetence—yet he had to hide his amusement before responding. "It's an interactive display. Kids are meant to fiddle with it."

"How was I supposed to know that?"

"It's your job to know."

She grimaced. "Good point."

Feeling like an ogre and wishing she'd stop worrying that delectably full bottom lip, he said, "You may have convinced my father to hire you for this job but I'm calling the shots now. And currently, I'm less than impressed with your performance. Your CV doesn't inspire me with confidence and neither have your skills on the first day."

She stood so swiftly he found himself reaching out to steady her, his hands connecting with her bare arms before he had time to think.

"Look, I'm just nervous, okay? This job means a lot to me and I'm sorry for the misunderstanding with that snotty-nosed brat—uh, little angel. As for the rest, I'll try to do better. Honest."

He heard the sincerity in her voice. However, it didn't match the banked heat in her eyes, and yet again he found himself contemplating the mysteries simmering beneath the surface of this vibrant woman—before mentally chastising himself to stay the hell away.

"Was there anything else? Because if there isn't you can probably let me go now."

He released her, unwittingly captivated by her warring vulnerability and defiance to the extent he'd forgotten he still had hold of her.

"A better effort is all I ask. So you're off to get that drink now?"

She shook her head, sending an intoxicating waft of peach and vanilla his way, instantly transporting him back twenty-five years to the rare indulgent days when his mom actually took time out to cook his favorite peach cobbler dessert.

"Bobby's not the patient type so he pretty much took off when I called him and said I didn't know how long I'd be here."

"Sorry," he said, not sorry in the least.

Though he had no right to feel this way, the thought of

her spending time with any guy, friend or not, in that sexy outfit, annoyed the hell out of him.

"How sorry are you?"

"Pardon?"

"If you're really sorry, you'll make it up to me by buying me that drink I've missed out on. I've had one heck of a first day, including being dragged in here after hours by a very demanding boss and being put on notice." She tilted her chin up and tucked a curling strand of strawberry blonde silk behind her ear, befuddling his senses with her sensual scent and quirking lips. "I'm stressed. I need to wind down."

He should've said no.

He should've cited work as a plausible excuse.

He should've remembered every sensible reason he had for pushing this woman away and not getting involved.

Instead, he found himself grabbing his car keys off his desk, placing a hand in the small of her back and propelling her out the door while trying not to grin like he'd just discovered Tutankhamen's forgotten tomb.

"Lucky for you, I'm in an extremely repentant mood," he said. "Let's go get that drink."

CHAPTER
FOUR

"Is this one of your regular haunts?"

Beth bit back a smile at Aidan's dubious tone. She'd been right in her assumption her stuffy boss wouldn't frequent a place like this.

Though that was unfair. Aidan wasn't all that stuffy considering she'd basically run a guilt trip on him earlier, not expecting he'd take her up on it. And not only had he gone for her idea, he'd been laid-back, witty, and charming on the way over here, regaling her with tales of his adventures overseas, making her all too aware of how downright appealing he was.

Much easier to think of him as uptight and not her type when in fact his adventurous side matched hers. She loved travelling too, loved exploring, loved finding hidden delights in places she'd never been, and hearing his stories only served to reinforce how much she needed to do well at this job so she could secure the gallery, make loads more money from selling her work, and indulge her passion for travel.

And doing well at this job meant not melting in a puddle at her boss's feet every time he smiled.

Trying to delude herself into focussing on 'stuffy' and not 'sexy' she glanced around. The Loft was packed to its steel rafters with patrons draped over the expansive mirrored bar, the low curved ruby sofas and each other, while funky acid jazz spewed out of floor to ceiling speakers designed to wake the dead.

"Don't worry, Professor, I'll look after you." She raised her cranberry martini in his direction while silently cringing for letting that little gem slip out.

His eyebrows shot up. "What did you just call me?"

"Professor," she mumbled into her drink, using the glass to shield her burgeoning smile at the frown creasing his brow and making him look more professor-ish than ever.

"Why?"

She waved away his question, sloshing some of her drink onto his leg in the process. "Oops, sorry."

She grabbed at the napkin serving as a coaster on the table and dabbed at the spreading gin stain on his pants.

"Leave it, it's fine," he snapped, stilling her frantic hand while she tried not to yank hers out from under his.

If she thought he looked hot, it had nothing on the effect he had on her body when he touched her. It had taken all her willpower back in his office not to lean into him when he'd taken hold of her arms in a purely reflex gesture, the type of rescuing gesture a guy like him would make.

She shouldn't have invited him for a drink. Flirting with the boss couldn't end well. What had she been thinking?

She hadn't, as usual, caught up in living in the moment. Story of her life.

"You didn't answer my question." He released her hand before taking a healthy slug of his boutique beer. "Why professor?"

"It's a term of endearment."

She raised her martini glass in his direction before draining the rest of her drink. Better to appear a lush than accidentally upend it over his chest. Though if she got a chance to dab at that broad expanse of muscle because of it...

His lips twitched, drawing her attention to their shape. They looked tailor-made for imparting instructions to his employees...or for kissing crazy women not doing a very good job when their dreams depended on it.

"But we hardly know each other. Not to mention I'm your boss and have bailed you up several times today, and you find me endearing?" He shook his head, a slow smile spreading across his face. "You're full of surprises."

If he bowled her over with his touch, his killer smile slugged her with its sensual power, and she cast a frantic glance at the bar, wishing it wasn't inappropriate to get tipsy in front of the boss on the first day.

"So tell me a bit about yourself, something I wouldn't know from reading your CV."

Twirling the delicate martini glass stem between her fingers, she decided to have a little fun. If the professor wanted her to do a better job, why not impress him with a little knowledge?

"I collect vintage hotties," she said, trying not to giggle at his incredulous expression.

"What?"

"You know, old hot water bottles made from porcelain."

As if. The only old stuff she collected came in crates, the bits of scrap metal essential for her unconventional creations. However, Lana collected old hot water bottles and she'd been drilled in the finer art of what a good hottie entailed, considering the museum had an extensive collection and she'd need to expound its virtues on her tours.

"Really?" By the sardonic quirk of an eyebrow, he was having a hard time believing her. "Tell me about them."

Wishing she hadn't drunk her martini in record time, she tried to recall every boring detail Lana had imparted, though she doubted her cousin had envisaged the cozy couch and drinks when they'd been practising the Q and A routine.

She certainly hadn't, and while she may have a razor sharp memory, sitting this close to him, trying to stay focussed on his eyes and not his lips, trying not to inhale for fear of copping another delicious lungful of the faintest ripe blackcurrant so reminiscent of her favourite Shiraz, it was increasingly difficult to string two coherent words together let alone recall boring facts.

"They date back as far as 1890. Of course they're not practical, made from porcelain and all, but I love their uniqueness. My favorite is a cylindrical foot warmer made by Lambeth Pottery in London, closely followed by a brown ceramic hot water bottle in the shape of a Gladstone medical bag. That one's made by Bourne Denby England. Then there's the foot warmer in the shape of a pillow which bears the word Osokosi, a play on the phrase 'oh so cosy'."

She slapped a hand over her mouth, pretending to shut herself up when in fact she couldn't remember any more of the facts she'd rote learned. "I can't help my enthusiasm when I start talking about my collection. I'm sure you didn't expect such a long-winded answer."

Something shifted in his eyes, a hint of shrewdness

mingling with confusion, as if he wanted to believe her but didn't.

"On the contrary, I'm fascinated by your hobby. Tell me more."

He was testing her.

She could see it in the triumphant glitter in his eyes, in the smug smile tugging at the corners of his mouth.

Too bad she'd run out of hottie facts to bore him senseless with. Or more precisely, she was bored out of her brain. He probably lapped up mindless drivel like this, considering he had to be fixated on old stuff to be an archaeologist in the first place.

Faking a trill little laugh designed to distract, she placed her glass on the table in front of them and clapped her hands together. "That's enough about me. What about you? Is there more to the professor than meets the eye?"

She half expected him to tell her to knock off the professor stuff but to her surprise he slugged back the rest of his beer before answering her.

"Not much to tell. I'm an archaeologist by profession who has temporarily traded in his trowel for a briefcase."

"Why?"

"My dad's unwell and asked me to fill in, though honestly? Living like a nomad has lost some of its appeal. I've explored the world, made my name, maybe it's time to try something else."

He spun the empty bottle in his hand, the expression on his face surprisingly somber for the discussion they were having. Since when did trading small talk get so serious?

"I'm a born and bred Melbournian, though haven't spent much of my life here, so when my dad gave me the opportunity to take over as CEO of the museum I grabbed it."

"Won't you find the stability boring after all that adventure?"

She certainly would. In fact, she couldn't think of anything worse than being stuck in an office job, compelled to enter the same building every day, cooped up in some dingy office, seeing the same people, doing the same tasks.

Give her the freedom of working from home when the mood struck, if her muse came out to play. Total freedom, just the way she wanted it, just the way she liked it.

"Do you find stability boring?"

Damn, he'd done it again, turning the spotlight back on her when it was the last thing she wanted.

"No," she said, wondering if it sounded like the big, fat lie it was before rushing on, "Surely you'll miss all that travel, the excitement of the search?"

He shrugged and placed the bottle carefully on the table, moving the coaster into place beneath it while hers lay scrunched in a used heap next to it.

"Time will tell, I guess."

Chastened by his downcast expression, she aimed to lighten the mood. "So what's been your biggest discovery?"

"I'd expect an expert tour guide like yourself to know all about that?"

The teasing glint in his grey eyes held her mesmerized and she sucked in a breath, his spicy scent packing as powerful a punch as the slow, sexy smile curving his lips.

She couldn't think straight when he stared at her let alone remember the question, and when he leaned forward a fraction and murmured, "Well?" she did the stupidest, most impulsive thing she'd ever done.

She kissed him.

WARNING bells clanged in Aidan's head as Beth closed the short distance between them and lay one on him.

A pretty pathetic description for the mind-blowing kiss to end all kisses.

The bells intensified as she placed her hands on his chest, bracing against him while angling her mouth for better access to his.

He had a split second to react, to come to his senses and stop this insanity. For that's what it was, total and utter madness, submitting to a scorching kiss from a sex kitten who happened to be an employee.

However, the moment her tongue flicked out to touch his, he threw caution to the wind and went crazy, dragging her into his arms, running his hands through the silky softness of her hair, savoring the sweetness of her mouth in a kiss that defied description.

He lost all sense of time and place as the kiss deepened to the point where she climbed onto his lap, slid her hands up his chest to anchor behind his neck, and hung on for dear life.

He would've lost it completely if not for the wolf-whistle from a nearby patron and he pulled away, a hint of cranberry on his lips and a handful of lush woman perched way too comfortably on his crotch. His very aroused crotch.

"I guess I should apologize for that," she murmured, her gaze uncertain, her expression half-dazed half-appalled as her tongue darted out to moisten her lips and he stifled a groan, desperate to pick up where they'd left off, knowing it wasn't going to happen.

He wouldn't let it, *couldn't* let it.

"I don't know what to say." He aimed for honesty, rather than some lame half-assed line like 'that was a mistake'.

Because it wasn't.

He may be a fool, he may be crazy, but he wasn't a hypocrite, and after spending all day denying there wasn't an ounce of attraction between them—and couldn't be because of their work situation—she'd blasted his reservations along with his self-delusions to kingdom-come with that scintillating kiss.

Sliding off his lap and smoothing her hair as if nothing had happened, she sent him another of those part-vulnerable part-seductress smiles.

"Then don't say anything. Let's just blame it on the atmosphere, the late hour, and the tension of interrogating your new employee."

Just like that, his passion-hazed mind cleared and clarity crashed in.

He'd just kissed his *employee*, when he'd always maintained a strict 'no mixing business with pleasure' rule his entire career.

Hell.

He had the best analytical brain in the business and whichever way he looked at it, what had just happened was wrong. He couldn't get involved with her, no matter how much she'd blown his mind with that kiss—or how much he'd like a repeat performance, taking it all the way.

So he was attracted to her? No big deal. He could handle it. As long as he didn't handle her.

He needed to get out of here, away from her intoxicating presence so he could think this through, but right now marshalling his thoughts was damn difficult considering the blood had drained from his brain and headed south courtesy of that incredible kiss.

"Blaming the atmosphere or the time isn't going to cut it. That kiss was way out of line."

"You're right." Her lips curved into a coy smile that had him focussing on exactly how great they'd felt gliding over his. "But it was sensational all the same."

She leaned toward him, her warm peachy fragrance wrapping him in a sensual cocoon as she whispered against his ear, "Just for the record, you kiss real good."

Unable to stop the goofy grin spreading across his face, and knowing he had to get out of here before he did something else he'd regret—or enjoy—he held up his hands in surrender. "I have to go. Early start tomorrow."

"Running scared, Professor?"

Her husky voice slammed into him with the same force as the teasing glint in those striking eyes the colour of dew-dampened moss, leaving him with the same floundering feeling he'd only experienced once before when a ton of sand had caved in on a site.

Now, like then, the breath squeezed from his lungs and he had no idea whether to struggle against the odds or give in to the inevitable.

For right at that moment, he knew he could struggle all he liked against the fierce attraction between them and he'd be powerless to stop it, just like he'd been unable to hold back that sand avalanche.

Ignoring her soft laughter, he shrugged into his jacket. "Come on, I'll take you home."

"I'll take a cab but thanks for the offer."

Her flirtatious smile would've tempted a saint, and considering the thoughts crowding his brain at the moment were far from heavenly, he needed to get out of here.

"Fine. I'll wait while you call one. Let's go."

She laid a tentative hand on his arm and he jerked to a stop, staring at her hand like it was a cattle prod. It had the same effect, giving him an electrical zap when he least expected it.

"This has been a bit of a crazy day for me all-round and I'm sorry for overstepping the mark back there." She ran her other hand through her hair and he yearned to do the same, to see if the luscious red-gold locks felt as silky as they looked. "I'm prone to doing impulsive things when I'm nervous."

Leaning forward until their noses almost touched, he murmured, "Do I make you nervous?"

Her eyes widened ad she inhaled sharply, her tongue darting out to moisten that full bottom lip he'd gladly taste again, and he had his answer before she spoke.

Dropping her hand, she stepped back and he stifled a sigh of disappointment.

"This job is important to me so yeah, after you virtually put me on notice earlier, I guess I am nervous."

There she went again, surprising him with that intriguing mix of bold bluntness combined with cautious hesitancy. He'd noticed how she'd changed the subject earlier, deftly switching the focus onto him, uncomfortable when he'd been delving into what made her tick, and he had the strangest feeling that her confidence was an act. Something—or someone—had put a susceptible chink in her sassy armor. What, or who, caused that vulnerable air that clung so delicately to her despite her bubbly façade?

He'd give anything to find out...but he wasn't going there, remember?

"So that totally explains why I kissed you." She gnawed on her bottom lip and clutched her bag tight. "Nerves."

"Uh-huh," he said, seeing the spark of desire in her eyes and not calling her on it.

There were more than nerves at play here.

She knew it.

He knew it.

"You'll see. I'll be back to my professional best tomorrow."

His lips twitched at the memory of her 'professional best' earlier that day. "I look forward to seeing that," he said, captivated by the earnest set of her mouth, the determined gleam in her eyes, and wanting more than anything to throw his business versus pleasure ideals out the window and haul her back into his arms.

"Good." She tilted her chin up, her defiance as enchanting as the hint of timidity he glimpsed beneath."Trust me, you won't be disappointed. I'll be the best damn tour guide you've ever seen."

"I look forward to that."

Unfortunately, that wasn't the only thing he looked forward to—just the thought of seeing her rock into the museum tomorrow was enough to put a spring in his step—and with a shake of his head, he propelled her out the door, determined to bundle her into a cab, head home, and lose himself in a mountain of boring paperwork.

Anything to take his mind off this intriguing woman and the memory of her scintillating kiss.

CHAPTER
FIVE

Beth bounced into work the next day humming an old song about getting a party started under her breath.

A tad late, considering it had well and truly started last night around the time she'd lost her mind and kissed Aidan.

And wow, what a kiss. As far as kisses went on a scale of one to ten, it scored a massive eleven.

She'd had Aidan pegged as a highly driven, career focussed, not much time for fun, type of guy.

She'd been wrong. Very wrong.

There was no way he could kiss like that if he spent all his time with his nose to the grindstone. Uh-uh. Aidan had depths to him she hadn't begun to fathom and boy, was it going to be fun trying to explore every hidden facet.

Yeah, he was her boss and yeah, she shouldn't go near him with a ten foot dinosaur bone, but that kiss last night had changed everything. She'd learned the hard way that life was too short not to make the most of every opportunity, and Aidan Voss was one big, delicious opportunity wrapped up in a designer suit.

"Hi, Beth."

She stopped at the tentative tap on her shoulder and swivelled to face Dorothy.

"'Morning. How are you?"

"Great." Dorothy tugged self-consciously at her burgundy fitted jacket flaring at the hips, over a matching pencil skirt. "Thanks for helping me choose this outfit yesterday. I feel like a new woman."

"You're welcome." Beth smiled, trying to focus on the suit and avert her gaze from Dorothy's staid navy pumps, whose scuff marks were poorly hidden by a shade of blue almost as hideous as the shoes themselves. "How about we do a bit of shoe shopping today at lunchtime?"

The young woman's face fell. "I can't. I'm filling in for one of the temps in the Science gallery."

"No worries, we'll do it tomorrow."

Dorothy's ecstatic expression made Beth glad she could share her love of fashion with her. "Sounds good."B

Beth glanced at her watch and grimaced. "Sorry, Dot. Love to stay and chat but the boss might be on the warpath."

Dorothy snapped her fingers. "I forgot. Mr. Voss wants to see you and he isn't looking happy."

"Uh-oh, what have I done now," she muttered under her breath, before thanking Dorothy and heading up to his office.

The solid, square heels of her new court shoes clomped along the marble corridor and she wriggled her toes in disgust, hating the fit of the ugly shoes almost as much as the look of them.

Though she was about to change all that.

She really shouldn't do this, considering she'd been trying to convince Aidan of her professionalism at the end of last night, but she'd seen the spark in his eyes, the devilish glint that told her their attraction was entirely mutual.

Besides, there was no harm in having a little laugh on the job. It fostered good workplace relations...it was team building...great for employee morale.

Smiling, she pulled up outside Aidan's door and cast a quick glance up and down the corridor. Reassured it was empty, she slipped a pair of fabulous mulberry spangly sandals out of her bag, kicked off the pumps, and reacquainted her feet with a familiar pair of old friends.

"That's better." Her grin turned positively smug as she admired the contrast of her hot pink toenails against the deep purple satin strap covering her forefoot. "Much better."

Schooling her face into serious mode was hard work considering the persistent smile threatening to break through as she envisaged Aidan's expression when he laid eyes on her shoes, but she managed it in time to knock sharply at his door and enter after his muffled 'come in'.

"You wanted to see me?"

She knew the exact moment he noticed the shoes. He stopped dead in his tracks half way across the office, his slate gaze riveted to her feet.

"What the hell are those?"

He pointed to her sandals and she wriggled her toes in response.

"Would you believe I had another shoe crisis on the way in today?"

His gaze snapped up to meet hers, stormy grey warring with cheeky green. "No."

"Would you believe the dog ate my work shoes?"

"No."

"How about I got held up by the shoe police for wearing such ugly shoes and to avoid being arrested I had to wear these?"

"You're pushing your luck." The corners of his mouth twitched, in total contrast to the frown marring his brow. "I told you to wear appropriate footwear today."

Unable to contain her laughter a second longer, she chuckled and slid the pumps out of her bag. "Relax, Professor, I was just teasing you."

His lips stilled and his expression darkened. "Like last night?"

Surprised he'd brought up the kiss, she perched on the edge of an overstuffed chair and swapped shoes. "Don't sweat it. I hope you didn't lose any sleep over what happened. I certainly didn't."

Checking out her shoes and wrinkling her nose at the come-down, she thrust the purple sandals into her bag and looked up at him from beneath her mascara-ed lashes. "As sensational as the kiss was, it's not worth losing sleep over. So, what did you want to see me about?"

She watched male pride war with indignation, knowing he'd be torn between discussing her flattery further and wanting to forget the kiss ever happened.

Sadly, it looked like his common sense kicked in and he walked around his desk and took a seat in an imposing leather chair that looked as uncomfortable as the one she sat on.

"There's been a change of plans."

He picked up a piece of expensive ivory paper that looked suspiciously like her CV and rattled it in her direction.

"I know you were going to spend the first few weeks conducting tours in the Australiana gallery predominantly, and helping out with organising a few workshops to familiarize yourself with the museum, but I need you to do more."

The bubble of happiness that sustained her through most days popped as the implication of his words sunk in. It had been hard work swotting up on all the info required to take tours of one gallery, imagine how much time she'd have to invest for more. And what with organising paperwork for the lease and completing her latest sculpture...this wasn't good.

He continued, oblivious to her escalating tension. "I think the quickest way to get you up to speed is to throw you in the deep end, and what with the flu bug hitting us hard at the moment and staff going down almost daily, I want you to take on the Aboriginal Centre and the Science gallery too."

Great. She may need this job to obtain the lease on her own gallery but what would be the point if she didn't have any pieces to fill it? She needed time to sculpt, but learning about these new areas of the museum at night meant she wouldn't have a free moment.

She'd have to tell him.

But what about her 'you can trust me I'll be the best damn tour guide you've ever seen' spiel she'd given him last night? If she backed down now and said she couldn't do it, would he chalk it up as another mark against her, or worse, fire her?

Clutching her bag to her chest, somewhat comforted by the stab of stiletto through the soft leather, she tried to think up with a quick-fire response. However, before she could come up with anything suitable, he handed her a bulging folder.

"Here. I know it's a lot to take in but I need you up to

scratch ASAP. You'll find information on those two galleries in here."

"When would you like me to start taking tours in the new galleries?"

"Tomorrow."

His direct stare unnerved her more than his unreasonable timeframe. For a fairly straightforward 'what you see is what you get' type of guy, his eyes glittered with triumph, as if he knew she couldn't fulfil her professional promise and had called her on it.

Floundering for something characteristically witty to say and coming up lacking, she gripped her bag tighter and opted for partial honesty.

"I appreciate your faith in me but I'm feeling a little overwhelmed, what with getting used to the one gallery, acquainting myself with the layout and staff and—"

"Either you can do it or you can't." He cut her off, his tone razor sharp and brooking no argument. "And if you can't...well, I guess we'd have to re-evaluate your contract."

Damn him. The laid back, sexy guy from last night had morphed back into the powerful CEO and she didn't like the change one bit.

As for threatening to fire her...no way she'd let that happen. Losing this job wasn't an option. And the potential fallout for Lana if she got retrenched...no, she couldn't even think about letting her cousin down.

"Of course I can do it."

Squaring her shoulders, she released her death grip on her bag, knowing she'd have to do some quick thinking to come up with a workable solution to this doozy of a problem. She may have a photographic memory but cramming in a folder's worth of tour guide expertise in one night would be impossible.

And Aidan would know it.

With a mental 'duh' it hit her. This was a test.

Maybe he really did want to get rid of her and was expecting her to fail spectacularly so he'd have no other option but to fire her?

Well, she had news for him.

She'd faced worse growing up from a father who'd pushed her to the limits repeatedly, expecting her to lash out, hoping he'd shove her away once and for all.

Instead she'd learned to shield her real emotions behind a confident front and a smart mouth, had practiced putting on a brave face while she hurt on the inside; the type of hurt that still lingered now, years later, the type of hurt that drove her every day to be nothing like him.

But she couldn't push her luck here. If this was some warped test she had no intention of failing. If it wasn't, maybe she could buy some time?

With a poised smile far removed from the jumble of nerves tumbling in her belly, she stuffed the folder it into her bag.

"I totally understand how tough it is around here at the moment with less stuff, but how about you give me a few more days to look over this and I'll start the new tours next week?"

The tiny crease between his brows reappeared, doing little to detract from his handsome face. "How many days do you need?"

"How about the rest of the week? That way, I can study over the weekend too and be up to scratch to wow the masses first thing Monday."

Sending him her best dazzling smile, she waited for a reaction.

He made her sweat for it, studying her face as if

searching for one of his precious old fossils, before allowing his lips to curve into a beguiling smile, the type of smile that could charm the pants off a girl.

If she were prone to that sort of thing.

"Fine, have it your way."

"Great." She leaped out of the chair, eager to make her escape while he was in a magnanimous mood.

"For now," he added, reasserting his power with the finesse of a businessman used to mixing subtlety with an iron clad will.

"Thanks, I'm sure you'll be impressed."

She hefted her bag with the ten-ton-tome of information under her arm and sent him a casual wave as she headed for the door, relieved he'd given her a reprieve. With a little bit of luck—and a lot of hard work—she could juggle her two jobs without letting any balls slip.

"I already am."

She turned at the door, the husky timbre of his voice alerting her to the fact that maybe, hopefully, he wasn't only referring to her work skills.

Sure enough, his gaze slid from her legs upward and she flashed a coy smile, buoyed by the gleam of male appreciation in those expressive silver eyes.

They may have dismissed that kiss last night as an aberration, but there was no denying the sizzle of attraction buzzing between them, professionalism or not.

"I can always slip the other shoes back on if you like?"

"For a woman perilously close to having me revoke those few extra days grace I've just given you, you're mighty sure of yourself," he said, grudging admiration in the hint of a smile.

"I know what I want and I know how to get it." She paused, letting her gaze drift to his lips before rising ever so slowly to reconnect with his smoky eyes again. "After last night, you of all people should know that."

Humming a song about kissing under her breath, she walked out the door.

∼

"Damn it."

Dorothy shot Beth a scandalous glance, as if she'd just dropped the F bomb. "Don't worry, we're only a few minutes late."

Beth practically ran the last few yards to the museum entrance, uncharacteristically grateful she wasn't wearing her stilettos for once. "I know, but I've got some snotty-nosed kids' tour group I have to lead."

And Aidan was tagging along to keep an eye on her.

That thought alone lent her extra speed and she flew through the door and waved to Dorothy over her shoulder. "See you later, Dot."

"Thanks for taking me shoe shopping," Dorothy called out, her wistful tone bringing her up short.

The young woman was a walking fashion disaster and Beth couldn't leave her hanging, not when she'd promised her a makeover to go with her new outfits and shoes.

"Look, I'm not trying to give you the brush-off, honest. I'll see you tomorrow and we'll tee up a time then for your makeover, okay?"

"Great." Dorothy's beaming smile could've lit a path for the space shuttle to follow. "I really appreciate what you're doing for me, Beth. You're the best."

If only Aidan thought so too.

Waving, Beth dashed into the Mind gallery, tugging down her jacket with one hand while tucking a stray strand of hair back into the bun at the nape of her neck with the other. She didn't know what was more annoying, the way the ill-fitting jacket kept riding up over her hips or the slight headache that came with wearing her hair confined in a knot all day.

However, with Aidan watching her every move during her first tour in this new gallery, she had to look the part even if she felt like the least qualified person on the planet to conduct it.

'Please let him be late,' she thought, her gaze darting around the room while she simultaneously managed a confident smile at the biology students waiting for her.

While the kids crowded around her, thrusting their hands in the air and firing questions before she'd even started, her gaze collided with a cool grey one at the back of the group, disapproval clear in its depths.

Great. Looked like the Punctuality Professor had already chalked up another black mark next to her name.

Determined to ignore him, she focused all her attention on the kids, who proceeded to make the next hour the most tedious, harassed, nightmarish sixty minutes of her entire life.

They hassled her. They laughed at her. One of the guys had the audacity to lay a hand on her butt as he pretended to jostle for a front position in the group.

If Aidan hadn't been around she might've been tempted to do something very unprofessional—like replace the human brain model with the real thing from that hormonal little creep—but she grinned, she extolled the virtues of the human body, and answered questions as best she could.

Which obviously wasn't good enough considering Aidan summoned her to his office when the tour ended. He didn't even have the decency to give her time for a recovery coffee.

"I'll see you in ten minutes," he said, tapping his watch as if she didn't know what it was or couldn't tell the time—okay, he had a point there considering she'd been late several times—frown in place, not a glimmer of a smile.

She nodded, too tired to respond, too despondent to fire back a witty quip.

This was it.

Her best wasn't good enough.

She'd failed Lana, and if there was one thing she took seriously it was being there for her cousin like Lana had been there for her all these years. And as she trudged the long corridor like a recalcitrant kid summoned to the principal's office, she couldn't think of one damn thing to do about it.

After pulling up outside Aidan's door, she knocked sharply, all business and no play, the exact opposite of her visit to his inner sanctum yesterday.

However, while she trembled inside, she wouldn't let it show. Brave front at all costs. It was a motto she lived by, a motto tried and tested many times when she'd craved one kind word from her dad and he'd ignored her instead.

Now, like then, she wouldn't let her nerves get the better of her. No good could come from appearing rattled. Her father had abhorred weakness and she'd learned to hide her insecurities at all costs.

"Brave front, show confidence, be humble," she mentally recited, and at Aidan's barked 'come in' she took a deep breath, entered the room and stalked to his desk, shoulders squared.

Determined to show no fear, she tilted her chin up. "What did you think of the tour?"

Admiration shot through Aidan as he stared at the pink-cheeked, unusually subdued woman standing before him. She'd be quaking in her boots, but apart from the faint blush staining her cheeks and the rigid posture, Beth showed little sign of being flustered.

He had a feeling what he was about to say would change that.

"Take a seat."

He pointed at the chair opposite, not surprised she sat quickly. For once he had Miss Fancy Feet on the back foot, no pun intended, and rather than feeling good about it, he hated what he was about to do.

But he had no other option. He couldn't have her here another day without wanting to drag her into this office, with work the furthest thing from his mind.

It had taken all his willpower not to haul her out of that tour and into the nearest janitor's closet to have his wicked way with her and he couldn't stand the tension any longer. Something had to give and unfortunately, it had to be her.

"Let's discuss your skills as a tour guide, shall we?"

She didn't blink or flinch or fiddle and his admiration went up another notch.

"I wasn't that bad." She eyeballed him, her bravado undermined by the slightest clench of her jaw.

"Actually, you're right. I could tell you'd studied the information I gave you last week, but unfortunately, it isn't enough."

He watched, transfixed, as she worried her bottom lip, and he folded his arms, tucking them in tight to avoid reaching out, tumbling her onto his lap, cuddling her close, and wiping away the glimmer of fear in her eyes.

"You're not a very tolerant man."

Her confidence impressed him. Even when faced with

impending dismissal she continued to dish it out to him. And rather than getting riled, he fought the impulse to applaud.

"On the contrary, I'm very tolerant. I've worked with people of different work ethics all around the world. I've worked through strikes, floods, even the odd plague of unwanted insects. But I must say I've never worked with anyone quite like you before."

"It takes all types to make the world go round."

"Correction, it takes all working types and that's one thing you're not quite up to scratch with, work."

Not entirely true. Beth may not know how to work as a tour guide to the standards he expected but she sure knew how to work it.

With every step she took, with every sensual swivel of her hips, with every toss of her head, and with every sexy smile, she knew how to work every gorgeous inch to her advantage, and from where he was sitting he sure as hell would miss watching her strut into a room.

Take today for instance. Who else had the confidence to stroll in late for a tour group, pretend he wasn't there, and then handle a bunch of hyperactive teenagers without losing control?

He'd been captivated from the second she'd locked gazes with him and proceeded to act as if he didn't exist, and while he'd been impressed by how much knowledge she'd crammed over the last week, it had been her natural exuberance that had more than made up for any shortfall in skills.

However, *joie de vivre* wouldn't let him sleep at night and he had to do this, despite how lousy it would be. Besides, he had a feeling that no matter how long she read up on the museum, Beth would be as far from a great tour guide as he was from his beloved Peru.

She attempted a haughty glare but it didn't work considering her eyes shimmered with disappointment and he fisted his hands to stop from reaching out to her.

The sassy Fancy Feet he could handle; her subdued, chastened counterpart almost undid him completely.

"I can assure you I know what hard work is, and if you'd give me a chance I can prove it to you. I just need more time to get up to speed so—"

"You've had your chances."

He hated her shoulder slump, the dejection lingering around her down-turned mouth, the same mouth that felt so incredible moving with innate sensuality beneath his.

Which is exactly why he couldn't be her boss any longer.

"Look, Beth, I can see you've tried and I admire that. But doing this job requires more than memorizing a bunch of facts and flashing a charming smile. I want someone with a genuine love for this place, for the displays, someone who can impart that enthusiasm during their tours. And while you're bright and bubbly and put in a huge effort, it's just that, an effort. I can't help but feel something's lacking. I'm sorry."

She gnawed at her bottom lip again, unwittingly drawing his attention to its plumpness, its softness, and the way it moulded so perfectly to his when they'd kissed.

"Well, looks like you've already made up your mind about me. Got anything else to say?"

Nodding, he watched realization dawn as her green eyes turned to flinty jade a moment before he said, "You're fired."

CHAPTER SIX

Beth exhaled, a long low breath that whooshed out of her lungs and sounded like a childish huff in the silence that followed Aidan's pronouncement.

"Just like that?"

"Just like that." He unfolded his long frame from the fancy leather chair and circled the desk to perch on it in front of her in typical alpha male pose, towering over her in an attempt to assert his power.

Well, she had news for him. She wouldn't bow down to any guy and as for quitting...that was for losers. She'd never quit on anything or anyone in her life; pity her dad hadn't felt the same.

"I wish I didn't have to do this but I have no choice."

Her gaze snapped to his, the genuine regret in his voice surprising. So he did have a soul.

"We always have a choice," she said, searching his face for some hint as to what he was thinking.

While she was usually good at reading people, she didn't have a clue what was going on behind those smoky grey depths at the moment. One minute he was the tyrannical boss booting her out on her butt, the next he sounded like he wanted to give her a comforting cuddle to make it all better. She wished.

"You don't have a choice in this case."

"Oh?"

Frowning, he swiped a hand over his face. "I can't discuss this with you. You have to leave."

The seriousness of the situation slammed into Beth with the force of a Melbourne gale. This wasn't one of the many times she could talk her way out of an untenable situation. This wasn't something she could laugh off, treat as another live for the moment life experience, and move on.

Uh-uh, this was her dream she was toying with, and Lana's reputation, with the potential to ruin both if she walked out.

She laid a hand on his arm and he jumped as if she'd electrocuted him, and as his gaze riveted to hers, she knew in an instant the real reason he'd fired her.

"It doesn't have to be this way, you know," she murmured, trapped beneath the burning intensity of his stare, her breath catching at the smoldering desire in his eyes.

"Yes, it does," he muttered, through gritted teeth, his yearning expression making a mockery of his words.

He didn't flinch or shrug off her hand when she slid her palm over the expensive cool wool of his designer jacket slowly upward until it rested on his bicep, the muscle flexing imperceptibly beneath her tingling palm.

"I know what this is all about." She hoped her touch conveyed that she understood, that he wasn't the only one caught up in this spellbinding attraction, that they could handle it even if working together.

"Maybe you do, but it doesn't change anything."

With a shake of his head he stepped away and turned his back on her to lean against his desk, arms outstretched, leaving her with a tempting view of his butt.

Oh yeah, there was definitely some major attraction going on and it wasn't one-sided. But where did that leave her? Jobless, with a huge crush on a guy she'd never see again when she left the museum?

There had to be a solution to this, a way they could work around it. He had to give them a chance...oops, she meant *her* a chance. Not walking out this door was all about work.

Yeah, right, and she could find her way around this monstrosity blindfolded.

Injecting lightness into her tone, she said, "Look, why don't we get out of here?"

"What?"

He swivelled to face her, his expression comical if it wasn't for the fact he could end her dream and any hopes she had of repaying the emotional debt she owed Lana with one quick word.

"Considering you just fired me I'd like to get away from this office, clear the air a bit, so why don't we go grab a coffee and have a chat?"

His jaw clenched, making the tiny muscle near the scar on his right eyebrow twitch, but his molten silver gaze hadn't lost the 'I want you but I'm trying to fight it' gleam.

"I don't want to do this," he said, his voice barely above a growl.

"I know you don't but it won't be too hard, promise. Just a little friendly conversation over the best cake you've ever eaten, accompanied by coffee to die for."

"You can't be referring to the cafeteria."

His wry smile showed her she had a shot at this, just as she suspected. For all his CEO bluster, Aidan was a bit of a softie beneath that tough, brash exterior, and if she could get him to face this *thing* between them, then reinstate her...

"Actually, I was thinking more along the lines of *Moretti's*."

"Never been there."

She pretended a mock swoon with a dramatic hand to the forehead. "You haven't lived in Melbourne before, have you?"

He shook his head.

"*Moretti's* is an institution. Come on, you have to try it. You'll thank me."

She stood and smoothed her jacket, her eagerness to get to the fabulous café having as much to do with clearing the air with Aidan in a guaranteed crowded public place as consuming the mouth-watering delicacies the place was famous for.

"You're the most exasperating woman I've ever met." He pushed off the desk with a resigned sigh, grabbed his cell and slipped it into his pocket before sending her a 'this better be good' glare.

"In that case, you need a great piece of cake. Quality cake is balm to a weary soul like yours."

"You're crazy." He shook his head while shrugging into his jacket, but she glimpsed the corners of his mouth curving into a fleeting smile.

She knew getting out of here wouldn't convince him to give her another chance but it was a start. And if she had to grovel, she'd rather do it while eating a delicious piece of cake.

"Okay, I'll admit it." Aidan's tongue flicked out to capture a stray cake crumb from his bottom lip. "You were right."

That one innocuous flick of his tongue derailed her temporarily and she struggled to tear her gaze away from his perfect mouth. If she wanted to jump him at the museum, it had nothing on her impulse outside of it, so maybe suggesting a visit to *Moretti's* hadn't been such a great idea after all.

She cleared her throat. "Told you so. Always trust a woman when it comes to good cake." Beth grinned before taking a bite out of a gigantic chocolate croissant, the flaky pastry melting on her tongue alongside the creamy custard filling. "So, is your soul soothed yet?"

Waving his fork at her, Aidan sent her a glare with all the force of a giant pussycat. "Only getting rid of you will do that, so start talking."

"Don't you want to finish your white chocolate mud cake first? What I have to tell you might give you indigestion."

"You've already done that," he muttered, his disapproval softening as he forked the last piece of cake from his plate into his mouth.

She knew nobody could stay mad for long while savoring a *Moretti's* delight. Maybe she should order him the entire mouth-watering display in the front counter considering what she was about to divulge.

After laying down his fork and pushing his empty cappuccino cup away, he folded his arms. "Now would be a good time to start telling me why you brought me here and what was so important you couldn't say it in my office."

She stuffed the last of the croissant into her mouth to

buy time, and held up a finger to ask for a minute. She was pushing her luck. But what the heck, he'd already fired her.

Which is exactly why she was here, to butter him up to take her back—or at the very least, beg.

Savoring the last silky slide of chocolate custard down her throat, she washed it down with a sip of latte before leaning back in her chair and trying her best beguiling smile.

"First up, I want you to promise that you'll hear me out."

A fine line appeared between his brows as he leaned forward, his face mere inches from hers. "You're in no position to make demands so cut to the chase."

She didn't move, momentarily captivated by the warmth of his breath fanning her cheek and the hint of coffee on his breath, knowing if she broached the short distance between them and laid her lips on his, he'd taste like the sweetest decadent white chocolate.

"Beth..." His warning growl roused her and she blinked, pulling away before she followed through on yet another insane impulse to kiss him.

Clasping her hands in her lap and schooling her face into a meek mask, or the closest she could manage to it, she said, "I'm desperate. Your father hired Lana Walker because she's the best in the business. My cousin is talented, dedicated, and one hundred percent committed to being the best curator the museum has ever seen."

His frown deepened. "And?"

"I can't mess this up for her. If I get fired, it's going to reflect badly on her."

"I'll make sure that doesn't happen." Shaking his head, he reached for his coffee before realizing it was empty. "Is that all you wanted to say?"

She dragged in a gulp of air, her lungs flooding with his sexy spicy blackcurrant scent mingled with aromatic coffee, and she knew it was now or never. She had nothing to lose. She'd already lost her job, what was a little pride chaser?

"No, I also wanted to say I'm attracted to you. And I'm guessing you're trying to push me away because the feeling's mutual and we work together and can't get involved. I'm also guessing we'd have a lot of fun together given half a chance."

He sat bolt upright as if she'd prodded him with her fork and she quickly continued before she lost her nerve. "I also think you're an adventurous guy. You'd have to be to have spent most of your life travelling the world, and you know something? Adventurous guys take risks. They take chances on things even though on face value they probably shouldn't. And that's what I'm asking you to do. Take a chance on me."

On us, is what she was really saying, and by the astute gleam in his eyes, he knew it too.

"You don't mince words, do you?"

She shrugged, thankful he was honest enough not to deny it. "What's the point? I've always been upfront, I say it how it is."

He ran a hand over his face before fixing her with that steady grey-eyed gaze that did delicious, tummy-tumbling things to her insides. When he wasn't busy firing her, that is.

"I could give you the brush off but that wouldn't be fair, considering you're right."

If her tummy had tumbled with a single look from him, it leaped and punched the air at his admission.

"So you're attracted to me?"

His rueful smile spoke volumes. "I think it was that kiss that did it."

"And don't forget the shoes." She leaned forward and whispered behind her hand, "You seem to have a thing for those."

His spontaneous laughter warmed her better than the fabulous lattes she always ordered here.

"So now that all this attraction business is out in the open, what are we going to do about it? And does this mean I'm not fired?"

His laughter petered out and he rubbed the back of his neck as if she'd given him an ache. Yep, that was her, a real pain in the neck when she wanted something, just like her dad had always said.

With her father, all she'd ever wanted was a little affection, some sign that he loved her, that he hadn't shut down completely after her mom died. Pity what Beth wanted she rarely got back then. Hopefully things would be different with Aidan now.

"You're right. Part of my rationale for firing you was because I didn't want to acknowledge this crazy attraction between us."

She batted her eyelashes at him, sending him a coy smile designed to tease. "And what's so crazy about it? I'm pretty cute, you know."

His genuine, easy-going smile transformed his face to drop dead gorgeous in a second. "Yeah, I know. That's half the problem. I can't seem to forget exactly how *cute* you are."

"And what's the other half of the problem?"

His eyes darkened to stormy pewter as he leaned forward and murmured, "How much I want you."

She sighed, desperate to close the short distance

between them and kiss him, to leap across the table and straddle his lap, to wrap her arms around him until he had no choice but to admit how fantastic it would be to give in to the heat searing between them.

"But we can't always have what we want," he said, breaking the spell by leaning back and folding his arms as if trying to ward her off. Like that would work.

She wriggled back in her chair and laid her hands palm-up in front of him, like she had nothing to hide.

"You know what I want?" Apart from him, but now wasn't the time to a articulate that, and she lowered her voice to math his serious tone. "I want another chance at my job. I promise I'll do better."

She held up a hand and pushed down a finger as she outlined her first point. "No more late starts."

His steely stare didn't encourage her.

She pushed down the next finger. "No more lunch-time shopping trips."

His eyes narrowed as she belatedly realized he probably didn't know about those.

The third finger went down. "No more slip-shod tours. I'll stay late, study hard, traipse from one end of the museum to the other to get familiar with the place, and I'll read every encyclopaedia-thick manual you throw my way. Twice."

His right eyebrow twitched, the scar beneath it doing a little dance.

Her pinkie joined the rest of her bent fingers. "Lastly, no more giving you a hard time. You've been really patient with me and I appreciate it, and I'm willing to do whatever it takes to hold down this job. If only you'll give me another chance."

She refrained from adding 'pretty please with a cherry on top', just.

No reaction. Not a glimmer of a smile. No amused glint in those slate eyes. Nothing.

In desperation, she grabbed a serviette off the table and twisted it in her lap, clamping her lips shut before she said something to blow her chances. She could plead her case further and tell him the whole truth, like how Lana was like a sister to her, how Lana was the only family she'd ever had after her mom died, how Lana had hugged her too many times to count when her dad wouldn't.

But what would be the point? Aidan was a facts guy. He dealt in a cold analytical world of black and white. He'd probably see her emotional side as a sign of weakness and there was no way she'd give him any more ammunition to get rid of her.

She'd done enough of that herself without trying.

When ten seconds stretched to thirty and the napkin lay shredded in her lap along with her fading hope, some of her old fire kicked in.

"Well? Are you going to keep me in suspense forever or do you want me to beg?"

Uh-oh, bad move. She bit the tip of her tongue as his eyes finally sparked. Had she really promised not to give him a hard time if he took her back? She had as much chance of following through on that as resisting a chocolate croissant every time she walked past this place.

Aidan steepled his fingers together and leaned forward, resting his elbows on the table. "When you said you wouldn't give me a hard time anymore, does that mean you'll stop calling me Professor?"

Before an instant agreement tumbled from her lips, he

held up a hand. "Because I've never had a nickname before and I actually like it."

Realization dawned in that moment.

She'd won.

He was giving her another chance.

"Thank you, thank you, thank you." Before she could think twice she jumped up from her seat, leaned across the table, framed his face with her hands, and planted an impulsive kiss on his lips.

She'd meant it as a thank you, a brief, impersonal, doesn't-mean-a-thing, kiss.

However, any sense of gratitude evaporated along with her plans to behave rationally as she registered the soft warmth of his mouth beneath hers, the feel of the faintest stubble against her palms, and the stimulating taste of coffee and chocolate lingering on his lips.

Knowing she had to pull away for the sake of her job she lingered a second longer, savoring the sensation of her mouth on his, before sitting again and fiddling with her hair as if the aberrant kiss had never happened.

Bracing for another warning, his warm smile took her completely by surprise.

"If that's what I get for reinstating you, I'd like to see what's in store if I give you a promotion."

Her heart kicked over at his power packed smile and the implication behind his words, while she wondered for the umpteenth time what it was about this guy that had her so hot and bothered.

He wore designer suits and sedate ties, she preferred jeans and T-shirts on her guys.

His hair was short and too tidy, she preferred long around the collar and unruly.

He was a CEO, she preferred creative guys, musicians and artists and writers, guys who didn't conform.

Then why couldn't she stop thinking about him let alone control her hormones? She heated from the inside out whenever he looked at her and as for their sparring...if he only knew how much a quick comeback and quicker wit turned her on.

Then again, maybe she was protesting too much? Maybe his latent adventurous side matched hers all too well? Maybe it scared the living daylights out of her how quickly she'd acted on their attraction? How much she'd like to take it further given half a chance?

More flustered than she cared to admit, she wriggled in her chair. "So I'm reinstated?"

Aidan watched Beth squirm, her hands shifting from fidgeting with the sugar sachets on the table to tucking stray strands of hair into her bun to toying with the cutlery.

He'd never met anyone so impulsive, so spontaneous, so downright amazing.

Even now he couldn't believe she'd been astute enough to figure out his rationale, then confront him about it, before verbalizing their attraction and having the audacity to ask for her job back.

Yet rather than being appalled, he silently applauded her bravado and her loyalty to her cousin. Her concern for her cousin's professional reputation surprised him. Not many people would care or make such a big sacrifice—like taking on a job totally unsuitable—for family.

He should know. His parents had never altered their schedules for him a day in their self-absorbed lives.

"Well?"

Her smooth brow puckered and he wondered if her skin felt as velvety-soft as it looked. He'd fantasized about how she'd feel ever since that kiss at The Loft the other night, though in his dreams he didn't just stop at feeling.

He imagined how she'd whisper his name as he caressed every inch of her body, how she'd moan as he tasted her, how she'd plead for more as she arched against him as he entered her...

"If you're going to make me wait for your answer, I guess it's not so bad if you look at me like that."

Snapping back to attention he stared at her, the faint pink of her cheeks and the knowing smile playing about her lips telling him she knew exactly what kind of effect she had on him.

Damn it, he shouldn't even be contemplating this. Taking her back meant more than just work and they both knew it. But he needed something in his life, a touch of exuberance, of excitement, something to make his blood fizz. The kind of thing that Beth had going on...in spades.

When she entered a room, everything seemed brighter. When she opened her mouth and dropped one of her typical gems, everything seemed funnier. And considering stepping into the CEO job for his father wasn't quite as satisfying as he'd imagined; he needed a spark in his life and that spark was Beth Walker.

Knowing what he was about to do was absolute madness but desperate to get some of his old enthusiasm back, he said, "Fine, you can have your job back."

One of her eyebrows formed a perfectly inverted V. "That's it? I've got my job back?"

"That's it."

Though it wasn't and he knew it. They both knew it.

There was no denying the chemistry between them any longer, especially as they'd both admitted it. And while he'd been a stickler in the past for not mixing business with pleasure, he now had no choice. He had to make an exception to his general rule, because his gut instincts screamed Beth Walker was worth it.

"Fantastic." She clapped her hands and beamed, her signature dazzling smile hitting him like a punch to the gut, leaving him winded.

When she smiled at him like that, it wasn't only sparks that shot through him but a cartload of fireworks, the whole damn exploding shebang.

"You're the best, Professor."

With her lips curved in a sassy smile, a cheeky glint in her sparkling eyes, and the lingering scent of peaches and vanilla clinging to his lapel where she'd grabbed him, he knew he was in way over his head. And loving it.

"Now that you're reinstated, I have a job for you."

"Name it." She snapped her fingers, all bright-eyed enthusiasm.

"Actually, it's not too arduous and doesn't involve carrying around any encyclopaedias of knowledge."

"Sounds like a piece of cake."

Her gaze drifted longingly toward the front counter brimming with baked goods and he briefly wondered if she was as passionate about anything else as she was for desserts.

Damn, he had it bad. He knew this would happen. As soon as he'd acknowledged their attraction, he couldn't stop thinking about getting physical with her.

Clearing his throat, he said, "It's company policy that the head curator accompany the CEO to the yearly fundraiser for the museum. It's a silent auction, pretty boring by all accounts, and seeing as your cousin can't make it and you're filling in for her tours, you'll need to step up. Think you can handle it?"

"No worries."

She sagged in relief and he chuckled.

"Let me guess. You thought I was going to ask you to clean Steggy."

Her brows creased into a cute frown. "Steggy?"

"The stegosaurus skeleton in the entry foyer. You know, that pile of old bones you walk past every day?"

"Oh, that." She waved her hand as if the priceless dinosaur exhibit was nothing. "No, I thought you were about to ask me to do something much worse."

"What's that?"

"Wear those standard issue flat shoes most of the staff wear." She wrinkled her nose and pursed her lips in a delightful pout as he clamped down the urge to kiss it away. "Have you really looked at them? They're hideous."

Shaking his head, he laughed. "Why do I get the feeling reinstating you is going to drive me slowly but surely crazy?"

Those entirely too kissable lips eased into a teasing smile as she leaned forward, creating a cleavage he struggled not to glance at.

"Don't worry. Whatever you're feeling, rest assured it works both ways."

That's exactly what he was afraid of.

CHAPTER SEVEN

Beth shoved the welding goggles up onto her head, shucked off her protective gloves, and wiped a grimy hand over her forehead, cursing under her breath as she stared at her latest creation in disgust.

The twisted pieces of iron resembled overcooked spaghetti rather than the spoked wheel she was aiming for, and though most of her pieces were uniquely quirky, this was taking it to extremes.

She'd never had a problem concentrating before. Then again, she'd never had a guy like Aidan Voss interested in her before, let alone be confident enough to admit it.

Guys liked to play games. They didn't do honesty well and they sure didn't verbalize how they were feeling, yet he'd been man enough to listen to what she had to say *and* confirm her suspicions. He fancied her. Hopefully, he fancied the pants off her.

The mere thought made her hands tremble and her insides throbbed as she pushed away from her work bench, knowing she couldn't shape a mud pie let alone mould metal the way her hands shook.

Something had shifted between them at *Moretti's*, something indefinable, and it left her wary. She could party and flirt and laugh her way through any situation, particularly when a good-looking guy was involved, but now Aidan had admitted he liked her, the underlying attraction between them wasn't so light-hearted anymore.

To compound her worry, she'd agreed to accompany him to a work function. All perfectly legitimate and aboveboard, except for one teensy-weensy fact: she didn't want it to be.

She wanted to go on a date with him. She wanted to flirt and tease and encourage that gorgeous smile of his until they were so hot for each other they had no option but to explore this attraction...all the way.

No surprise why her own work was suffering, considering she couldn't think of little else.

Groaning, she switched off the welder, placed it on the work bench and stood, clasping her hands and stretching overhead, letting her head loll forward before rolling the kinks out of it. Giving Lana an abbreviated version of events was going to be stress-inducing enough without the normal muscle tension that accompanied her beloved metal sculpting.

Casting one last look at the heap of junk she'd managed to construct in the hope of getting her mind off things—or one particularly sexy thing—she picked up her cell and tapped number one in her favorites list. Predictably, Lana answered on the second ring.

"Hi, Beth. How's it going?"

"Good." She deliberately turned her back on her disastrous sculpture, a reminder of exactly how things were going; a twisted, jumbled mess. "How's the ankle?"

"Coming along, I guess, but not quickly enough for my liking. How are things at the museum?"

Beth squeezed the bridge of her nose, hoping she could pull this off. If Lana got one whiff of the trouble she'd got into, her cousin would ditch the crutches and hop all the way to Beth's warehouse apartment to give her a swift kick in the butt with her good leg.

Instilling her usual enthusiasm into her voice, she said, "Fine. I'm still taking tours and it looks like I'll be expanding into some new areas of the museum too."

"Great." The relief in Lana's tone was audible. "I can't believe you're actually buckling down. I thought being a tour guide would be the last thing you'd want to do."

"Hey, nothing to it." If she didn't count getting busted for punctuality, getting fired, and getting a pseudo-date with the boss. "I'm even going to some museum function this weekend so I'm really wowing them."

"What sort of function?"

Doing her best breezy impression, Beth sat on a nearby sofa and dangled her legs over the end. "Nothing major. Just some silent auction fundraiser. Apparently it would be your job to accompany the CEO but you're off your feet so I'm going instead."

She omitted the part where she wished the CEO would whisk her back to his place afterward and do some very un-work-like things with her.

"Uh-oh. You're humming, which means you're nervous, distracted, or hyped up about something."

Beth quickly clamped her lips shut, unaware she'd been indulging in the habit of a lifetime. "Nope, not hyped or distracted here. Humming means I'm happy." Or trying to give the illusion of it while she tried not to contemplate spending an entire evening as Aidan's platonic date.

"Okay, I'll play along, but if you're humming, I'm worried."

Damn Aidan Voss for getting under her skin.

"Give me a break. All that cramming I'm doing to make sure I'm a fab tour guide and your reputation as a gun curator stays intact is probably taking its toll."

Lana laughed. "You know I'm grateful, especially now I know you're actually doing this. But remember, even though it's a work function, act professional, okay? I know how much you love a party and you can't afford to fraternize too much, especially if you're accompanying the boss."

Beth grimaced, imagining what Lana would think if she knew exactly how much she wanted to fraternize with the delectable Aidan.

"No fraternising here, I'm a professional." She crossed her fingers behind her back with her free hand. "I have to go. Look after that busted ankle."

"Shall do. Have fun at the function, but not too much."

Beth forced a chuckle, trying to ignore the instant image of Aidan that sprung to mind when she thought of having fun. "Okay. Bye."

After disconnecting, she placed the cell on the work bench and rolled her shoulders again. Maybe she was making too much of a big deal about this. Aidan was just another guy and this was just another function.

Yeah, right.

She yanked her protective goggles back into place, shoved her hands back into gloves, and picked up the welder.

Time to set off some real sparks in more ways than one.

AIDAN PULLED up outside the derelict old warehouse in the heart of Brunswick and silently cursed the Sat-Nav in his car.

One look at the grubby grey walls, peeling red paint on the solitary door, and the deserted street told him he must've punched the wrong address into it.

'So much for satellite navigation,' he thought, reaching for his cell to check the maps app, and the piece of paper with Beth's address. However, a brief glance at her bold, flowing script told him he hadn't made a mistake and neither had his car's equipment.

She lived in this run-down, eerie warehouse.

Surprised, he got out of the car and strode to the door, curiosity lending a spring to his step. From the minute he laid eyes on her he'd known Beth was something else and she'd continued to intrigue him with every passing day, and now this.

With her flair for fashion—when not at work—and sassy attitude, he'd pictured her inhabiting some trendy city apartment, living the good life: parties, dancing, café culture. Instead, she chose to live in a dingy Brunswick street in a warehouse that wouldn't look out of place in a vampire flick.

Brunswick may be one of Melbourne's cosmopolitan inner suburbs but none of the gloss had reached this place yet. Hitting the intercom button, he waited. And waited. And waited. He was just about to reach for his cell when the red door opened with a flourish and his mouth went dry.

"Hey there, Professor. Ready to leave?"

It had been worth the wait as he started at the top, admiring her loosely arranged reddish-blonde hair piled on top of her head before his gaze slid down her body, taking in the silver shimmery dress skimming her body like liquid metal poured on and ending inches above her knees, the long expanse of bare, bronzed legs, and another pair of 'take me' shoes.

Leave? Was she kidding? With her in that outfit, a coy smile flirting around her mouth, and a mischievous gleam in her eyes, he didn't want to leave, he wanted to push his body up against hers, back her into the warehouse, and have mind-blowing sex. Wild, passionate, unrestrained sex, the type of sex he'd been fantasizing about ever since he caught his first glimpse of her long legs.

"Nice shoes." He wrenched his gaze up to meet hers, the faintest hint of peach beckoning him to close the short distance between them, take hold of her, and capture her mouth with every ounce of barely restrained desire pounding through his body.

It had been way too long since he'd had the time to date, and the enforced celibacy that came with being the best damn CEO the museum had ever had, had him on edge.

"I aim to please." With a husky laugh that resurrected fond memories of sultry heroines from the classic black and white movies he liked, she shut the door and slipped her hand around his elbow. "Now, let's go wow these stuffy geeks at the fundraiser."

Just like that, some of his good mood evaporated. Was that how she saw him? As some stuffy professor-ish type who didn't know how to have fun? He had to know.

"Am I included in the stuffy geek brigade?"

Her eyes glittered with amusement as she laid a hand on his shirt and it took every ounce of willpower not to capture it and drag the rest of her into his arms.

"You are definitely not stuffy geek material," she murmured, her palm smoothing an imaginary crease slowly, sensually, notching up the heat between them and making him grit his teeth with the frustration of not having her naked and panting. "You're way too adventurous for that."

"Adventurous, huh?"

"Oh yeah."

Her tongue flicked out to moisten her bottom lip, almost undoing his weakening resolve as he rested a hand on her hip, savoring the feel of hot skin through the slinky fabric of her dress, wishing he could watch it slither down her gorgeous body.

"You're beautiful," he murmured, trapped in a sensual cocoon of her warm peach fragrance, the spark of desire in her eyes, and the secrets in her smile.

"And you're the most charming guy I've ever met."

Her hand slid downward to rest on his hip as they stood there for an eternity, locked in each other's stare, their bodies so close, but not close enough.

"Charming, huh?"

"Yeah," she said, on a soft breath, her eyes conveying a message he hoped he wasn't misinterpreting.

"You know we have to go, right?"

She nodded, her hair draping her shoulders in shimmering spun gold. "Maybe you can charm me some more later?"

"It's a promise," he said, reining in his urge to say, 'to hell with later,' and, taking hold of her hand, he led her to the car.

The faster he did his duty at the fundraiser, the faster he could get to 'later'.

BETH HAD NEVER BEEN the clingy type. When she arrived at an event or party, she liked to make an entrance.

However, the minute she stepped out of Aidan's car in front of the elaborate entrance to the Massey Hotel and he offered her his arm, she'd been more than grateful for the support.

This evening would be full of surprises, starting with Aidan discovering what the lead item in the auction was.

If she hadn't been nervous enough about that, seeing him dressed in a designer tux, charming smile in place, and touching her hand with ease as if he squired flirty females to fancy functions every day of the week, would've set her nerves jumping anyway.

"That's cute," he said.

"What is?"

She clutched his arm a tad tighter as they entered the foyer, her heels clicking on the highly polished marble as the reflected light from a stunning chandelier momentarily dazzled her; only slightly more than the sexy man staring at her with a quizzical expression.

"You were humming under your breath."

"I always hum. Lifelong habit. My dad used to say there's a song for every occasion, I guess he was right."

He paused and steadied her as they stepped off the top of an escalator. "He used to say?

"He died when I was eighteen."

Almost to the day, as if he'd waited until she could legally do everything for herself before pegging out. Pity he hadn't done a thing for her emotionally while he'd still been alive.

She expected a trite 'I'm sorry.' Instead, Aidan said, "Do you miss him?"

Good question. Shame she didn't have the faintest clue how to answer.

"Not really. My mom died when I was six and my dad virtually shut down after that. We weren't that close."

"Families, huh?"

She glimpsed pity in his eyes as he tried to make light of her admission and it annoyed her. She didn't need his pity. She didn't need anyone's pity. She'd done a fine job taking care of herself all these years and, apart from Lana, she knew better than to depend on anyone, especially some guy who thought he could breach her defences her with smoldering grey eyes and a sexy smile.

"It sounds like you have a family tale of your own to tell," she said, determined to deflect his attention away from her morbid past.

She noticed the slight tightening around the corners of his mouth, the tenseness in his jaw, though his smile didn't waver.

"Not much to tell, I'm afraid. My folks are both historians. They traveled the world while dad fueled his archaeological habit before he took over as CEO of the museum. He ran it for twenty-five years before asking me to step in."

"Keeping it all in the family," she said, surprised by the flicker of bitterness in his eyes.

"I guess."

They reached the entrance to the ballroom where the auction was being held and a round of introductions to a group of people she had no hope of remembering stalled any further probing on her part.

For that's exactly what she'd been about to do, delve into Aidan's past. He had a story to tell, she could sense it. What better way to gain insight into the guy than by discovering his background. Besides, it was much more fun than dwelling on her family life—or lack of.

"Want to check out what's on offer?"

"I already have." Her gaze perused the length and breadth of him before sending him a coquettish look from beneath her lashes.

He laughed, a low rumble of pure joy that sent a thrill through her. "See anything you fancy?"

"Oh yeah," she murmured, mentally moving his butt to the top of her very own gropeable list. "Though I'm not sure if it's in my price range?"

The fine hairs on the nape of her neck snapped to attention as he leaned closer, his breath fanning her cheek.

"There's only one way to find out. Why don't you put in a bid?" His deep voice sent a ripple of desire through her. "You never know, you might get lucky."

Everything faded away—the muted light from wall sconces reflecting off sequinned designer dresses, the soft classical music filtering from a high-tech sound system, the drone of voices from a thousand people—as his lips brushed her cheek in the lightest of touches, so light she could've imagined it—or willed it, more likely.

Caught in the heat of his stare, the spicy blackcurrant undertones of his aftershave invaded her senses and she struggled not to close the short gap between them and do what she'd wanted to do since their first memorable kiss—a repeat performance.

"Get lucky, huh? I'm counting on it," she whispered as his fingertips slid up her arm, skimming her bare skin like the touch of the flimsiest butterfly wings taking flight.

"If this evening wasn't so damn important for the museum I'd say let's ditch this place."

Stifling a sigh of disappointment at his CEO conscientiousness, she tapped his cheek lightly. "Don't worry. The night is young."

His scorching glance set her body tingling all the way down to her metallic blue toenails poking from her silver spiked stilettos, but before he could say anything else a guy bearing a striking resemblance to an archaeologist in a movie she'd seen as a kid, complete with battered hat, bore down on them and practically dragged Aidan away.

Grinning at his pained expression, she sent him a jaunty wave and headed for the front of the room where a roped off area kept curious buyers away from the more expensive items.

Professional pride filled her as she stared at her latest triumph, a mini version of the Sydney Opera House, her very own interpretation of the iconic landmark.

"The least you could've done is rescue me," Aidan said, behind her. "You're supposed to be supporting me, remember?"

Beth turned to Aidan, surprised he'd returned to her side so quickly. "I didn't think you needed rescuing. After all, don't you CEO types need to mingle and schmooze and generally suck up to people?"

He frowned, as if her teasing hit too close to home. "You're right. CEOs do have to do that sort of thing, which is why I'd rather spend the bulk of the evening with you."

A warm glow filled her. Apart from the sizzling attraction between them, she genuinely liked him, and what had looked like a novel way to secure her lease and hold down Lana's job at first glance was fast turning into something far more important.

She may be a fling type of girl but right now her heart gave a scary twang, the type of twang that said she could seriously fall for this guy if she let go.

Flustered by the uncharacteristic surge of emotion clogging her throat, she gestured toward her sculpture.

"What do you think of this piece?"

He screwed up his eyes, tilted his head to the right, then left, before taking a step back and repeating the process. "Not my sort of thing. Too modern."

The tender emotion of a moment ago melted away as she absorbed his critical expression and came to a startling realization.

His opinion mattered to her.

He'd hurt her.

Which could only mean one thing: she could be falling for him.

Desperate to ignore the surge of panic telling her to make a run for it while she still could, she forced a laugh. "Of course it's too modern for you, considering you've spent half your life rummaging in the dirt looking for old stuff."

Something in her tone must've alerted him to the fact she wasn't as unaffected by his opinion as she'd like to be, because he captured her chin in his hands and tilted it up gently until she had no option but to stare into his gorgeous grey eyes.

"What's up?"

"Nothing."

She lowered her gaze before he read the lie there, only to be confronted by his equally gorgeous lips, lips that felt exceptionally good plastered against hers.

"This isn't the time or place," he said, in a voice like smooth velvet as he skimmed his thumb along her bottom lip before releasing her as if he'd been burned. "But trust me, if you look at me like that later tonight, I won't be held responsible for my actions."

Grateful they'd slipped back into flirting mode, she quirked an eyebrow and tapped his chest with a French manicured fingernail.

"Haven't you heard? Being responsible all the time is highly over-rated."

Flecks of speckled cobalt flared amidst the dreamy grey depths of his eyes as a confident smile curved his lips. "I'm all for forgetting my responsibilities for a night."

She splayed her palm on his chest, absorbing the heat radiating through his dress shirt before sliding her hand down and tucking it around his elbow as if that had been her intention all along.

"And I'm all for being the one responsible for you forgetting. But don't we have an auction to attend first?"

Muttering a curse, he tucked her hand closer and headed into the ballroom at a half-run.

She laughed. "If you're in such a hurry because you can't wait to get me alone later, I like the way you think."

He stopped dead and she bumped into his side, relishing the all-too-brief contact of one half of his body slamming against hers.

"I'm hoping you'll like a lot more than that." He slipped a protective arm around her waist as his enigmatic gaze sent a thrill of anticipation through her. "In fact, I'm counting on it."

Beth couldn't think for a moment, what with his hand nestled comfortably around her waist, his thumb strumming back and forth, and the intent in his eyes notching up her excitement levels to unbearable.

Moistening her bottom lip with her tongue, and enjoying the fleeting tortured expression that flickered across his face, she murmured, "The faster you bid, the faster we get to the good stuff."

With a muffled groan, he released her. "Come on, quit dawdling."

She chuckled, the confident sound of a woman who knew what she liked in a man and how to get it, as Aidan all but dragged her into the ballroom in a fair imitation of a sedate sprint.

CHAPTER
EIGHT

As they pulled up outside Beth's warehouse and Aidan parked, he couldn't help another disgruntled muttering.

"You should've told me," he said, as they walked toward the front door, a vibrant crimson that hurt his eyes even in the dim street light.

Beth unlocked her front door and pushed it open, shooting him a mischievous glance over her shoulder, accompanied by a toss of her silky blonde hair. "Why? I knew you'd find out soon enough."

Shaking his head, Aidan followed her into the cavernous warehouse, hoping the inside was a lot more inviting than the bleak exterior.

"I certainly did." He blinked as she flicked on switches, flooding a suspended wooden walkway in light. "Unfortunately, I get to find out that my newest wannabe tour guide is actually a star sculptor when I see her name on the program, and how much her art is worth rather than hearing it from the sculptor herself."

She chuckled, the throaty, full-on laugh he'd grown way too fond of way too quickly.

"It's your fault. I was going to tell you before you wrinkled your uppity nose at my best work in ages and said it was *too modern*."

His mouth twitched as he feigned indignation. "There's nothing uppity about my nose and I definitely didn't sound like an R&B singer on steroids when I said it was *too modern*."

'Unfortunately,' he thought considering most women were into that soul-deep crooning voice thing, as he followed her down the walkway before stepping down a small flight of stairs into a room the size of a small aircraft hangar.

She laughed and crooked a finger over her shoulder, beckoning him to follow. Like he needed to be asked twice.

"This is some place." He spun a three-sixty, taking in the eclectic mix of rippled steel ceiling, white-washed stone walls, honey-coloured wooden slat blinds over monstrous windows, and the largest, brightest splashes of paint passing as pictures hanging on the walls at various spots throughout the warehouse.

"I like it." She headed into a tiny kitchenette at odds with the size of the rest of the place. "What would you like to drink?"

"Coffee's fine. Black, one sugar thanks."

He headed over to a spot-lit corner featuring a giant Japanese screen inlaid with the finest mother-of-pearl cherry blossom motif. It was a work of art and he couldn't help but run his fingertips over the exquisite craftsmanship.

Damn, he missed field work, missed the excitement of searching, the thrill of discovering ancient items of beauty.

Things like this screen were made for the world to appreciate, yet the closest he got these days was staring at priceless pieces behind the glass of a museum cabinet with the rest of the public, rather than touching and feeling and experiencing the sheer rush of finding a beautiful artefact.

"If you like the screen, what until you see what's behind it."

She joined him, handing over a mug of steaming coffee before stepping around the screen and jerking her head to indicate he should follow. "This is where I work. Though I guess it's not really your thing, being so *modern* and all."

"Give a guy a break," he said, sipping at his coffee, wondering whether the jolt of energy coursing through his veins came from the caffeine rush or the sight of Beth picking up pliers and a shiny sheet of steel, caressing the metal with the kind of touch she'd reserve for a lover.

"I'll think about it."

He loved her impudent smile as she gripped the metal with the pliers and twisted it into a star with origami-like precision.

"You're very talented." He drained his coffee and placed the mug on a sideboard before joining her at the workbench. "What's the real reason you didn't tell me about all this?"

Her hands stilled, the pliers appearing surprisingly delicate resting in her palm despite their size and function as she raised her eyes to meet his.

"Because you were having too much fun putting me into a nice, neat box, organizing your opinions like you do the rest of your life."

"Where did that come from?"

Though he had a sinking feeling he knew. She was brash, funny, exuberant; and obviously thought he was the opposite considering her nickname for him. She thought he was a pedantic workaholic who couldn't have fun. Sadly, she was right. He never used to be that guy but he was these days and for what? To prove something to a man who probably wouldn't notice if he danced naked on top of the Sphinx?

When she didn't respond, he sat on a stool next to her and picked up a miniature wrought iron basket. "On second thoughts, don't answer that. Being your boss, coming down heavy on you and all the discipline that goes with it hasn't given you a very good impression of me, huh?"

She gnawed on her bottom lip and he struggled to ignore the surge of lust at how much he'd like to do the same.

"Actually, you've been pretty great about everything."

"But you think we're too different."

Hell, he'd probably reacted to her work exactly how she thought he would. Though she didn't say the words, he remembered her disappointment when he'd commented on her showstopper at the auction before she'd masked it with her usual quick wit.

"Not really," she muttered, lacking total conviction, and he stood and drifted toward a nearby bookcase constructed from twisted metal and glass, grasping at a change of subject before he was sorely tempted to prove to her how similar they could be.

Scanning the shelves, the strange mix of anatomy and psychology texts next to classic literature surprised him.

"Bit of light reading?"

She swiveled to face him, wariness clouding her eyes. "Just some stuff I read in my teens while trying to figure out what I wanted to do with my life."

His eyebrows shot up. "You read anatomy textbooks in your teens?"

She shrugged and fiddled with the pliers, twisting a metal sliver into a pretzel. "I was gifted."

She dropped the bombshell in the same monotone a kid might use to request a peanut butter sandwich.

"Let me get this straight. Your IQ is off the charts, you could be anything you want, and you choose to play with metal for a living?"

He knew it was the wrong thing to say the instant the pliers sheered off and sliced the metal clean in two.

Damn it, he usually weighed his words as carefully as his decisions, but somehow her announcement had thrown him more than discovering the wrought iron impression of the Sydney Opera House at the auction tonight was her creation.

She picked up another sheet of metal and resumed twisting with the pliers, and he had the distinct feeling she was wishing it was his head.

"I like what I do, I like being creative," she said, her voice glacial, her eyes shooting green fire. "What I don't like is feeling constricted or being confined when I could be out and about getting inspired for my work."

She stabbed at the metal, making a giant hole for goodness knows what reason. "I also don't like being judged by the size of my brain."

She paused to give a particularly vicious twist to the metal to the point where it bent and contorted to breaking point. "And I really, really, don't like some judgmental jackass like you belittling what I do."

She was right. He didn't take her job seriously and hadn't from the first moment he'd learned the truth tonight.

Mentally kicking himself for being such a moron, he crossed the room to stand in front of her, willing her to look at him again, to pay as much attention to him as she was to the bizarre creation in her hands.

"You know what I like?"

"What?" She lifted her head a fraction, enough for him to see her frown while her body language—folded arms, tense shoulders, slight lean away from him—screamed hands off.

Like he could do that.

"You," he said softly, cupping her chin, using the gentlest of pressure to lift her face toward his, hoping she'd listen to what he had to say after the way he'd blundered through things the last few minutes. "I like you. I'm sorry I offended you. You caught me off guard, that's all."

Her compressed lips softened a tad but she didn't lose the frown. "It still doesn't change the fact you think I'm wasting my time being a metal sculptor rather than using my brain for something more worthwhile. Like an archaeologist perhaps? Or maybe a brain surgeon? Or a rocket scientist?"

She snapped her fingers. "I know, maybe I should be the world's greatest tour guide/curator."

Her frown vanished, accompanied by a twitching of the corners of her lush mouth. "Oh, that's right. I already am."

To his amazement, she laughed, a loud, belly laugh that echoed in the cavernous warehouse, bouncing off the walls until it enveloped him with her natural spontaneity and warmth.

"So I take it I'm forgiven for being a conservative jackass who can't think before he speaks?"

"There's nothing conservative about you."

Her eyes widened to large green pools as his hand slid

from under her chin to rest at the nape of her neck, as if she anticipated his next move would be to draw her closer and kiss her senseless.

"Just in case, I think it's time to shake things up a bit, to show you exactly how non-conservative I can be."

Aidan didn't know who made the first move but the short space between him and a handful of luscious woman vanished in an instant as they lunged at each other.

"Never knew you could lighten up this much, Professor," she gasped as he slid his hands over her shoulders, pushing down the flimsy straps holding up her shimmery, barely-there dress as he'd been yearning to do all evening.

"There's a lot you don't know about me, Fancy Feet," he murmured, savoring the feel of silky soft skin beneath his fingertips, blazing a trail with his lips where his hands had just been.

A weird sound somewhere between a snort and a laugh erupted near his ear. "Fancy feet?"

He raised his head from the creamy skin of her neck reluctantly, muttering a curse. "Not the most romantic endearment you've ever heard, I bet."

She smiled, a sensuous upward curving of her lips that had him dying to cover them with his own. "I've heard better. Then again, it is original."

"It's those damn shoes you keep wearing." He pointed to yet another sexy ensemble designed to entice and make him focus on the perfection of her endless legs. "How's a guy supposed to not ogle your sensational legs when you draw attention to them with shoes like that?"

A little furrow appeared between her brows. "Hmm... you have a thing for shoes. You haven't got some weird foot fetish, have you?"

"There's nothing weird about how much I enjoy

admiring your feet and the way they attach to your very sexy legs."

He slid his arms around her waist and pulled her close until she couldn't mistake the bulge in his pants for anything other than what it was, irreversible proof of exactly how much he desired her.

"I guess not." She smirked and wound her arms around his neck, pulling his head down toward her. "Now that we've established how much we like each other with the nickname thing, where were we?"

"Right here." He settled his lips over hers, more than a little disconcerted at how right it felt.

Like he'd finally come home.

Like this was the type of woman he could get used to having around for longer than his usual few dates.

He deepened the kiss, pure, unadulterated lust shooting through him as she matched him thrust for thrust, her tongue winding around his, teasing, tasting, taking as much as she gave.

He groaned as her hands grabbed his butt, hanging on as if she couldn't get enough, while her mouth left his to nibble her way across his jaw to his ear where she bit hard enough to brand him as hers, soft enough to leave him begging for more.

"Bedroom?" he managed to grit out as she slid a hand around from his butt to cup his erection, sending the blood roaring through his head as she shifted her hand up and down the length of him.

"Now, now, where's your adventurous spirit?" She sent a pointed look at the plush red rug beneath their feet and he grinned, more than eager to dispense with the wasted seconds it would take to reach her bedroom.

"I like the way you think." He tugged on the zip holding

up the silver sheath, smiling when it gave a satisfying hiss and the dress pooled in a glittering heap at her feet.

"That's a mighty confident grin," she murmured, not in the least embarrassed as his gaze left her face to slide downward, his breath catching at the sight of her beautiful breasts. Full. Round. Exquisite.

Unable to keep his hands off them a second longer, he cupped them, savoring their lushness, skimming a thumb over each pale brown nipple. "That's because I'm guessing we're a sure thing right about now?"

"Good guess."

She drew his belt out of his pant loops inch by inch, deliberately brushing against his erection with every move. Torturing him, teasing him, her touch driving him slowly but surely crazy.

He usually liked to take things slow, to draw out the pleasure, but with every tantalizing touch he knew he'd combust if he didn't follow his basest instinct and have fast and furious sex with this feisty woman who could turn him on with the barest hint of a twinkle in her incredible eyes.

As if sensing his need, the next few moments were a blur of fast hands, flying garments, and clashing mouths as they repeatedly kissed while tearing each others clothes off, the air filled with her soft pants and his heavy groans.

"At last," he murmured, as she stood before him, naked, glorious, her shy smile hitting him where he least expected it: his heart.

His *heart*?

Hell, it really had been way too long since he'd had sex. Since when did he let himself feel anything beyond job satisfaction, let alone let emotion into his life? Emotions were wasted. They built hopes and fuelled dreams before disintegrating into the dust he used to dig through.

He'd learned it as a boy, had it confirmed as a man, and there was no way he'd let Beth get too close no matter how much he wanted her.

"Come on." She tugged him down to the rug and he quickly banished his thoughts to concentrate on the task at hand; losing his mind with the woman who turned him on with a simple smile.

Beth moaned as Aidan's lips trailed down her neck, hard, insistent, creating heat and sending rivers of mind-numbing need flooding through her body.

"Oh..." She arched upward as his mouth clamped around a nipple, sucking, nipping, teasing her with his skilful tongue while his hands were free to roam south, skimming her belly before gently spreading her thighs.

"Am I going too fast for you?" He lifted his head as she let out another hearty moan and she chuckled.

"What would you do if I said not fast enough?"

His eyes darkened to pewter as his lips curved into a naughty smile, a smile loaded with wicked promise.

"I'd do this."

With a fast move she'd associate with a porn star rather than a CEO he flipped her around, his hot breath fanning against her stomach and bringing his arousal in her direct line of vision.

"Slick move, Professor, very slick," she murmured, a second before he placed his mouth against her throbbing centre, sending sparks of electricity shooting through her body in little bursts of pleasure.

"Fast enough for you?" He spread her further apart, his tongue finding her clitoris with unerring accuracy, licking at her, flicking her in quick darting movements designed to send her into orbit in the blink of an eye.

"Oh yeah," she said, through gritted teeth, wondering if

there was a world record for the fastest orgasm ever, sure she was about to beat it with the help of one very sexy guy.

He paused, his glance scorching. "We've done it your way for a while, now we do it mine."

She made a tiny mewl of disappointment, her pelvis making a small unconscious thrust up toward his mouth, shamelessly begging for more.

"You may like things fast but us staid museum types prefer it slow." He dipped his head to lick her once, twice. Long, drawn out sweeps with his tongue that had her biting her lower lip to stop from crying out. "Real slow."

"Slow is good too," she managed to say before he picked up where he'd left off, though this time at a much slower pace that drove her wilder than before.

Closing her eyes, she gave in to the sensations bombarding her, making more noise than was polite for a first time with a guy but not giving a damn. Blinded with mindless need, her head dropped forward, only to be nudged by the hard evidence of what her rather shameless noises were doing to him.

"Payback time..." She leaned forward a fraction to take him in her mouth, enjoying the tortured groan he let out as she licked him with the same fervor he was inflicting on her.

"Too much," he muttered, picking up where he'd left off for a second, driving her to the brink of losing control.

"On the contrary, not nearly enough." She raised her head to send him a seductive smile.

She'd never felt this empowered, this confident, and it had everything to do with the guy about to send her to the moon and back with the best orgasm of her life.

However, before she could resume her ministrations, Aidan did some weird circular thing with his tongue once, twice, and she shattered, her inner muscles clenching, her outer muscles dissolving as she came apart on a loud scream.

Smiling, he shimmied up to join her, caressing her cheek with an unbearable tenderness in his eyes. "Please tell me you don't live in this place without a neighbor within a block because you regularly make sounds like that."

"Fine, I won't tell you." She planted a lip-smacking kiss on his mouth while sliding her hand down the hard planes of his stomach, savouring the feel of smooth skin, the rasp of hair below his navel arrowing downward. "But just for the record, I chose this location for the workshop space, not for the lack of nosy neighbors who might have a hankering to listen to noises that don't occur very often anyway."

Considering he'd just given her the orgasm to end all orgasms, the triumphant, gloating, all-male glint in his eyes didn't surprise her. He was good, damn good, and he knew it.

"Good to know," he said, his hands stroking her back in slow, sweeping movements until she almost purred.

"Now, before you get too conceited—and yes, the noise I made definitely corresponds with how amazingly talented you are with your tongue—it's time to return the favor."

Grinning like the smug male he was following the ego trip she'd just sent him on, he grabbed his pants, withdrew a condom from his wallet and sheathed himself quickly before laying back, hands folded under his neck, elbows out, the epitome of a guy who knew he was smoking-hot and how badly she wanted him.

"I'm all yours. Go ahead, do your worst."

"That's some challenge," she murmured, straddling him in a second, enjoying the desperation that flickered across his face as she brushed his erection with her slick entrance.

"Lucky for you, my worst also happens to be my best." She slid downward, inch by torturous inch, until he filled her completely, revelling in the feel of him inside her, the anticipation building all over again as she began to move up and down.

"You're incredible," he ground out as he grasped her waist, matching her pace, thrusting up as she slid down, his heated gaze never leaving hers.

Beth always had to have the last word and could usually come up with a quip in a second. However, with his every thrust she coiled tighter inside, the tension rebuilding until she could do little but hang on for the ride.

"Oh yeah..." His guttural groan heralded her own release as stars danced before her eyes and she collapsed on top of him, her body turning into a sensual puddle of stimulated nerve endings and mushy muscles.

Shifting slightly beneath her, he cradled her head, lifting it until he could look directly into her eyes.

"You just blew my mind," he said, slanting a slow burning kiss across her lips, the kind of kiss that had her wishing she did more than date a guy for longer than a few months.

"Same here."

He kissed her again and again, soul-drugging, toe-curling, mind-blowing kisses designed to take her on an erotic journey to a record number of orgasms in one night.

Humming the faintest strains of a classic song about sexual healing under her breath, she gave herself over to enjoying what promised to be the best night's sex of her life.

CHAPTER NINE

"What's going on?"

Beth stopped chopping onions and dashed a hand across her teary eyes, squinting at her cousin propped in the kitchen doorway.

"I'm making you my world-famous lasagne, that's what. Personally, I think you're taking this whole invalid thing a tad far. I'm betting you ditch the crutches the moment I'm out the door and dance around here naked."

Lana quirked an eyebrow and stared down at her baggy brown cords, shapeless beige sweater, and scuffed lace-up boots, her usual conservative stay-at-home garb. "You think?"

Beth laughed, wishing Lana would let her give her a make over. It might help Lana to loosen up, act her age, have a little fun, maybe go the whole hog and find a guy. "Well, maybe not. Now, vamoose. You have a master chef at work here."

Lana shook her head and hobbled toward the island bench where she propped on a stool. "Sorry. Not leaving until you tell me what's up."

"All this lazing around has given you an overactive imagination. There's nothing wrong."

Beth resumed dicing, needing to keep her hands busy and her mind focused on getting the recipe right; anything to keep her mind off the extremely X-rated fantasies—though they could officially be classed as memories now—of Aidan.

Lana picked up a wooden spoon and banged it on the side of a stainless steel cookie container. "Spill it. You only ever make lasagne as comfort food and you've just hummed the entire repertoire of every eighties band from that easy listening playlist you obsessively play. So time to 'fess up. Something's wrong."

Turning away from Lana's probing stare, Beth winced at what she was about to do. Considering her cousin would have to work with Aidan once her ankle healed it was only fair she told her the truth. Besides, Lana had been her confidante, best friend, and sister rolled into one forever and Beth was busting to tell her what had gone down—literally—with Aidan.

After rinsing her hands under the cold tap and drying off, she turned back to face Lana, who was patiently staring at her with a quirked eyebrow. Beth drew out a kitchen chair and pointed to it.

"You better sit down. I have a feeling you're going to need to when you finish hearing this."

Concern bracketed Lana's mouth in an instant. "Are you okay? It's nothing serious?"

Beth sat on the chair opposite Lana and said, "Depends on your definition of serious. If you think sleeping with the boss is serious, well then, it's—"

"You did *what*?" Lana sat bolt upright so quickly one of

her crutches toppled and slammed against the floor with a bang.

"It's no big deal, really," Beth hurried on, more than a little intimidated by the appalled expression on her cousin's face. "We've had this flirting thing going on from the start and we kinda got carried away after that silent auction fundraiser and—"

Lana shook her head and held up her hands. "Whoa. Tell me this is yet another example of your warped sense of humour. Tell me you didn't really sleep with Aidan Voss."

Beth tried to keep a straight face and failed. She couldn't, because the instant Lana mentioned Aidan's name she couldn't keep the satisfied smile off her face.

"Okay, I didn't sleep with Aidan Voss...considering there wasn't much sleep involved."

Lana groaned and dropped her head in her hands. "This can't be happening."

Banishing thoughts of how fabulous the minimal sleeping she'd had with Aidan had been, she sobered up for her cousin's sake.

"Look, it's not that bad. We're both consenting adults, it's not really going anywhere, and once I'm out of the museum it'll all be forgotten."

Lana's head snapped up as she pinned her with an accusatory glance. "But what if it doesn't end well? Where does that leave me, my job?"

Beth lowered her gaze, preferring to trace the chocolate brown and aqua circles on Lana's fifties tablecloth rather than face the blind panic in her cousin's eyes.

Lana's sharp intake of breath sounded like a clap of thunder in the growing silence. "What else have you done?"

Knowing Lana wouldn't buy her best innocent look—she never had, all those times Beth had swapped book reports, 'borrowed' her best jewellery, pilfered the last of her favorite chocolate bar—she tried one on for size anyway.

"He knows how important your job is. I made sure he understands that."

"You made sure he understands that..." Lana parroted, before bolting upright for the second time in as many minutes, her face turning scarlet. "Why? What have you—"

"Settle down, Cuz. I reinforced how important your reputation at the museum is to keep my job after he virtually fired me, but everything's cool now."

Extremely cool, considering how they'd blown each other's minds last night.

After several deep breaths that restored her color, Lana said, "Okay, I'm not even going to ask why he virtually fired you, because I still have my job." She tapped a split fingernail against her bottom lip before shouting, "Then what on earth possessed you to sleep with him?"

"Would you believe the devil made me do it?"

Beth couldn't help her response and she sure couldn't control the smile tweaking her lips.

Ever since they were kids she'd been making Lana laugh, trying to lighten up her serious cousin, trying to make her see that life wasn't all textbooks and museums.

Thankfully, Lana was usually a good sport and the minute her tight-lipped, grim expression softened, Beth knew she'd be forgiven.

"You're nuts, you know that?"

Beth shrugged and picked up the pitcher of iced tea she'd set out earlier, pouring them both a generous glass. "Like you didn't already know."

Lana accepted the proffered glass, the rim barely hiding her growing smile. "You actually slept with Voss the Boss," she murmured, shaking her head before taking a healthy slurp.

"And you're actually lightening up enough to call him that?"

She met Lana's bemused glance and they burst out laughing.

"I guess it's pointless me asking how good he was?"

"You can ask, I just won't tell you." Beth hoped the instant heat flooding her body at the memory of her night with Aidan didn't make it to her cheeks. "Besides, you're the workaholic. Think how awkward it could be at your first staff meeting, trying to maintain a professional front when you know how long his—"

"Point taken." Lana almost snorted the remainder of her tea before her smile faded and she leaned forward, pushing her glasses up her nose and reverting to her usual serious mode. "Just don't screw this up for me, okay? You've been amazing helping me keep my job but I know you. Just be careful."

"Of what?"

Lana paused, as if searching for the right words, before blowing out a long breath that sent her scraggly fringe heavenward.

"You date a lot of guys and pretend to be the ultimate party girl but I know for a fact you don't sleep with many of them. And I've got to say I'm pretty surprised you're even interested in Aidan considering he's probably not your type."

Beth frowned, still none the wiser about her cousin's warning.

Was she trying to tell her to take care of her feelings or Aidan's?

"You're being as clear as mud. Come on, spit it out. I'm a big girl, I can take it."

Concern flashed in Lana's eyes before she blurted, "If Aidan's anything like the usual museum crowd, he's a stayer. He's the type of guy who expects more from a girl than a one night stand."

"Who said anything about a one night stand?"

It certainly wouldn't be, not if she had anything to do with it. She had more than a few weeks left of strutting her stuff as a tour guide and she had every intention of making every second count.

She may not go in for the whole long-term commitment thing but who said she couldn't have fun while it lasted?

Lana topped up her glass and took a long sip before answering. "We both know the longest you date is three months before moving on. And we both know why."

Her heart sank. She should be on a high after last night. Instead, here she was playing twenty questions with her nosy cousin and having to suffer her amateur psychobabble to boot.

"This has nothing to do with my folks." She kept her tone deliberately flat, downing another top up and leaping from her chair. "Now, I really have to finish this bolognaise sauce if you want to eat any time this century."

Lana wouldn't push. She knew it, Lana knew it. It had always been the way with them: Beth the confident, outspoken one, Lana the shy, retiring one who gave her opinion but wouldn't force an issue no matter how right she was.

"Fine. I just care about you." Lana's soft spoken words hung in the air and Beth blinked several times, grateful her back was turned.

"Right back at you, Cuz," she said in a fake, perky

falsetto, resuming her chopping at a frantic pace in an attempt to drown out any further forays into topics she'd rather not discuss.

Pity she couldn't drown out her thoughts, especially the main one centred around a very ooxy boss and the strange urge to do something completely out of character...like let him hang around for longer than the requisite ninety days.

~

BETH FOUND herself humming on Aidan's doorstep before quickly silencing her vocal cords.

She'd never been this nervous and it was all Lana's fault. So he'd invited her to dinner at his place? No big deal. But ever since Lana had planted the idea of Aidan being a stayer in her head, she'd been as fidgety as her cousin that time she'd offered to dust her precious tea cup collection.

Beth didn't do relationships.

Never had, never would.

Commitment led to dependence, dependence to devastation when that person eventually left, and there was nothing surer. If the love of your life didn't walk out on you, they upped and died eventually anyway, leaving you emotionally crippled for life and she had no intention of being hobbled for anyone.

Yeah, she was excessively cynical. Though she'd rather be a realist than one of those romantics who believed in soulmates. She never saw the point in setting herself up for failure.

The door opened and she fixed a smile on her face, more than a little disconcerted a family of butterflies had taken up residence in her stomach. Worse, they took flight the second she caught sight of Aidan in casual gear for the first time. He wore a navy T shirt, faded denim, and a sexy smile.

"Hey, Beth. Any trouble finding the place?"

Dragging her gaze away from his chest, which appeared so much broader in soft cotton than the stiff business shirts he usually wore, she sent him a flirtatious glance from beneath her lashes.

"I'm here, aren't I?"

"You sure are."

She propped in the doorway, enjoying his leisurely perusal, wondering if he approved of her outfit as much as she did his.

"Nice shoes." His sizzling glance implied the avocado satin ankle-tie-ups she'd taken an eternity to choose were a hit.

"Enough with the shoes fetish already."

She rolled her eyes in mock exasperation as she slid past him, planting a casual kiss on his cheek as if having dinner with the guy she'd had sensational sex with the night before was something she did every day.

"Anything you say, Fancy Feet."

She smiled, still not quite believing he'd given her a nickname. He'd appeared so uptight when they first met, and while the nickname was dorky and old-fashioned, it was kinda cute.

In the short time she'd known him, he'd surprised her on many levels; especially with the inventive talents he'd exhibited last night, and the thought alone made heat rush to her cheeks.

"Something smells great." She inhaled deeply as she followed him up a short hallway and into the most bizarre kitchen she'd ever seen, with its old versus new motif: ultra mod stainless steel appliances clashed with an antique dresser, the black granite bench tops out of place next to an old Agar stove.

"It's one of my foolproof recipes, from a limited repertoire I might add," he said, lifting a pot to release a fragrant aroma of lemongrass and coconut into the air that made her mouth water. "Hope you like Thai chicken curry."

"Love it."

She slid the bottle of chardonnay she'd brought out of her bag and placed it on the granite-topped bench before pulling up a stool, afraid of how domestic Aidan appeared, the comfortable atmosphere between them, and how much she liked it.

"I'll pop the rice on then we can relax in the other room," he said, looking way too efficient as he measured out the jasmine rice, the water, added a pinch of salt, and added the lot to a rice cooker.

Apart from lasagne she could barely make a cup of tea and adding culinary expertise to Aidan's growing list of talents wasn't helping the stayer versus fling argument in her head.

"There, all done." He wiped his hands on a dishcloth hanging on the oven door handle, giving her a prime view of his butt as he bent forward. "Now, for some wine..." He trailed off as he stood a lot quicker than anticipated and caught her perving on him, a slow smile spreading across his face. "Or would you prefer something else?"

Ignoring the way her heart pounded at the thought of 'something else', she handed him the bottle of wine.

"As much as I fancy dessert, I'll settle for wine now."

His eyes glittered with fervor as he registered what she meant. She hadn't counted on getting horizontal by the end of this evening, but seeing him look at her with potent desire told her exactly how much she was kidding herself.

She had as much chance of resisting him as taking some monotonous desk job somewhere: absolutely none.

She wanted him. Naked. Gloriously naked. Skin on skin. With her.

Beth wasn't sure how long they stayed that way, gazes locked, the heat sizzling between them having little to do with the curry simmering on the stove, but she was the first to break the deadlock before she flung herself over the island bench and tackled him to the floor.

"Interesting place." She swiveled on the bar stool away from his assessing stare, willing her heart to stop pounding like a temp with a crush on her first boss.

Though what hope did she have, with Aidan propped against one of the bench tops, looking sinfully delicious, more so than the chocolate mousse she'd glimpsed when he opened the fridge.

"This place belongs to my folks. I'm crashing here for a while."

She couldn't fathom the strange look he got every time he mentioned his family, an almost furtive guilty expression that darkened his eyes with pain.

"Mom wanted the appliances though goodness knows why as she rarely cooks. As for all the plates and other paraphernalia, she's a hoarder from way back. Collecting old stuff goes with the territory of being a historian."

Bemused by the cynicism in his voice, she tucked her feet under the stool rung and wriggled until she was comfortable. "Considering your job, you must be into old stuff too. What do you collect?"

He paused, sending her a wicked grin that curled her toes. "Hotties, just like you."

Twirling a strand of hair around her finger—wishing she could do the same to him—she leaned forward and lowered her voice. "I'm guessing you're not referring to the ceramic type."

"You mean like your extensive collection?"

They laughed, as Beth wondered how she'd ever thought she could convince him she was conservative.

"You know, Lana actually does collect ceramic hot water bottles."

"Really?"

She nodded, surprised by the swift stab of jealousy at the sudden interest in his eyes, glad when his gaze dipped to her cleavage briefly before returning to her face, scorching in its intensity.

"Personally, I'm into hotties that collect shoes."

He pushed off the bench top, his biceps bunching impressively as he strode across the kitchen and offered her his hand, his smile giving those damn butterflies in her stomach a new lease on life.

"Come on, I'll give you the grand tour."

"Is this your less than subtle way of getting me into your bedroom?"

Heat pooled in her belly at the thought as she slipped her hand into his, powerless to resist this sexy guy at his flirting best.

He wiggled his eyebrows suggestively, the action so ludicrously exaggerated she laughed. "No, it's my way of taking my mind off exactly how hot you are and stopping myself from getting down and dirty with you right here, right now."

"Oh," she managed to say as all the air whooshed out of her lungs, and as she took a deep breath his spicy scent mingled with the fragrant cooking aromas, making her mouth water more than ever.

"Let's go before I change my mind and lose the chivalry

act." He nuzzled her neck, sending shards of pleasure through her body and she sighed out loud when he pulled away.

"You didn't have to go through all this trouble to get me into bed," she said, gesturing at the stove top, the wine, and the cozy table for two set in the corner. "I'm a big girl. I don't need all the trappings."

His right eyebrow shot up, the small scar adding to his comical surprise. "Where did that come from?"

She knew. She'd known the instant she set foot in this room and seen Aidan looking so comfortable, seen the results of his culinary efforts, the easy way he treated her, a heady mixture of light flirtation with innuendo.

This entire scene was too seductive, but not in a sexual way. Seeing him like this, relaxed, contented, casual, scared her more she'd anticipated.

Sharing a home cooked meal, having him lavish attention on her with the seductive promise of so much more, was terrifying to a girl who never did this sort of thing, to a girl who couldn't think beyond tomorrow let alone contemplate more than a few dates with the same guy.

Her stomach churned, her heart flipped, and her palms grew sweaty, physiological responses to a psychological problem she was all too aware of.

She didn't do intimate dinners with dates for this very reason.

She dated guys who went to loud parties, dance clubs, and who wouldn't know coriander from a blade of grass.

She dated guys who had the same expectations as her: none.

She dated guys nothing like Aidan.

So yeah, she knew exactly why she'd spelled it out for

him that she didn't need romancing, but there was no way she'd tell him.

"Sorry, didn't mean to bite your head off. I'm just not very good at all this couple stuff."

His grip on her hand tightened as he tilted her chin up to stare deep into her eyes. "Maybe you just need practice?"

She gulped, captured by the heat radiating from him like warming rays from a welcome winter sun, terrified he'd virtually verbalized her greatest fear: he wanted more from this—thing...fling...whatever she wanted to pass it off as—than she did.

Breaking the hypnotic eye contact by stepping back and swinging their linked hands like a preschooler, she said in an all-too-bright voice, "Let's take a look around."

To his credit he didn't push her for answers despite the curiosity clouding his eyes, and tugged her toward the door.

"Living room." He pointed through a door on the left and she darted a quick glance around, taking in the pine floorboards, Persian rug, tatty cream sofa, crammed bookshelf, open fireplace fanned by a gold peacock guard, a model of an old steam ship, and a mantelpiece adorned with several rather ugly statues and figurines, immediately struck by how different this was from her place.

Old versus new, antique versus contemporary. The contrasts served to reinforce the yawning gap between the two of them. Aidan versus Beth.

The thought saddened her more than she thought possible for a carefree type of girl.

"This is the den."

She peeked through the door and spotted more antiques, crammed bookshelves, and old paintings.

They strolled the corridor to the next open door.

THE BOSS

"Spare bedroom," he said.

She barely gave the boring beige room a glance, increasingly nervous as they reached an ornate door at the end of the hallway that had to lead to the master bedroom.

"My room," he murmured, with the faintest hitch in his voice.

Closing her eyes for an instant, she pictured black satin sheets, ruby red scatter cushions, and mirrored ceilings.

A girl could fantasize, couldn't she?

"It's not that scary."

His amused tone alerted her to the fact he'd sprung her daydreaming.

"Says you. For all I know you probably have a fully equipped dungeon in there."

His eyebrows shot up and she laughed at his horrified expression.

"Relax, I'm kidding. Somehow, I can't see you as the bondage type."

His eyes darkened with mystery and she swallowed, all too aware of their proximity and the fact there was probably a bed with their names written all over it behind the door.

"I'm not. Though the odd silk scarf or two might come in handy..."

Her breath caught as he slid an arm around her waist and drew her close, slanting a slow burning kiss across her lips, the type of kiss designed to stoke her fire, a kiss that turned her into a quivering mess with the barest flick of his tongue against her lips.

"Have you ever been tied up?" He whispered against the corner of her mouth, his breath sweet from the chardonnay, his piquant aftershave with a hint of blackcurrant intoxicating.

Her eyes fluttered shut as he kissed his way toward her ear lobe, and the instant they closed she could envisage the two of them in vivid detail: naked, her lounging back on satin sheets, Aidan over her, tugging gently on purple silk binding her to a wrought iron bed...

"You don't have to answer if it makes you uncomfortable." He pulled away as she opened her eyes to find him staring at her with concern.

She chuckled, not surprised her laugh had a slight hysterical edge considering she couldn't get the erotic image of the two of them and those sexy silk scarves out of her head.

"I'm not uncomfortable, it's just that your question about being tied up during sex surprised me, considering you're the quiet charmer and I'm supposed to be the bold one, remember?"

He winked as he threw open the door. "Haven't you heard the quiet ones are always the worst?"

"I stand duly warned," she said, exhaling as she glimpsed the bedroom, not sure if she was disappointed or relieved at the lack of satin sheets and silk scarves.

However, her imagination took flight again as he led her into the most gorgeous room in the house, a room at complete odds with the rest.

"The ensuite," he said, in the same conversational tone he'd used to announce the rest of the rooms.

"Wow." She released his hand and headed straight for the monstrous spa bath mounted in the corner. "This is amazing." She let her hand drift along the pale green marble, the gold taps, the border edged in exquisite mosaic. "You must never want to get out of this."

He propped in the doorway, amused at her drooling over a bath tub. "Actually, I've never taken a bath."

THE BOSS

"Here, you mean?"

He shook his head, joining her at the tub. "Ever."

Aidan saw the confusion in her eyes and felt compelled to explain. "My mom and dad made me shower as soon as I could stand up. Guess they never had the time for lolling around in baths."

She snorted. "By the looks of this tub I'm guessing they've changed a lot since then. This is one serious bath tub."

He shrugged and perched on the edge of it. "Personally, I don't see the attraction."

"You're kidding." With a snap of her fingers, her eyes lit up and she yanked open the vanity cupboard, ducking her head into it and letting out an excited squeal.

Covering his eyes with his hand, he said, "Don't tell me, you've found more evidence my folks aren't the couple of old fuddy-duds I imagine."

Straightening so fast she almost hit her head on the washbasin, Beth faced him with a cheeky glint in her eyes and a teasing smile playing about her mouth. "Don't worry, there aren't any silk scarves if that's what you're worried about."

He groaned, quickly blotting out that ghastly image. "You've got a dangerous look in your eyes."

She advanced toward him, sashaying across the incredibly large bathroom. "Dangerous, huh? Perhaps you should be afraid."

She hooked her hands around his neck and pulled him down for a swift, scorching kiss that had all the blood in his head instantly heading south. "Very afraid."

He needed little encouragement to prolong the moment, his excitement skyrocketing as she opened her mouth to him again, her tongue slowly meeting his in an erotic, sinuous dance that had him wishing they could stay like this forever.

Forever?

In that moment it hit him, how much he'd like to get to know this crazy woman, every gorgeous, spontaneous inch of her, and how much—for the first time in his life—he'd consider staying in one place for an emotional reason rather than for his precious career.

Buoyed by the startling realisation of how much he wanted a relationship with her, he backed her against the vanity cabinet, kissing her longer, harder, deeper, hungry kisses that fuelled his fire for her.

"Mmm..." Her appreciative moan sizzled through his blood and he almost lost it.

However, this wasn't what he wanted from tonight. At least, not until later, after he'd wined and dined her, chatted and flirted with her, establishing a connection that went beyond the incredible physical bond they shared.

Last night at her place had been amazing and he'd replayed it like a porno through his mind all day. But he wanted tonight to be about more than sex, about exploring the possibility of the two of them dating, and hot on the heels of his revelation a few moments ago, he knew he had to take this slow despite every horny cell in his body telling him otherwise.

Ending the kiss with reluctance, he pulled away just enough to trace her lips with his finger, to watch her shining green eyes haze over with passion.

"I need to check the stove before my efforts to impress you go up in smoke."

She smiled, trying to draw his finger into her mouth but he was too quick, snatching it away before she undid him completely. "You've already impressed me and it has nothing to do with your cooking skills."

Battling a raging libido was hard enough without this sexy woman staring at him like she wanted to eat him alive, but he managed to take a few ragged breaths before stepping away.

"How about we eat first and do some serious searching for those silk scarves later?"

Her answering smile, laden with promise, had him thrusting his hands into his pockets—what little room was left—to stop from reaching out and grabbing her.

"Deal. Though you have to promise me one thing."

"Anything."

Leaning closer, her breasts brushed against his chest with exquisite torture, a second before she whispered in his ear. "You give me ten minutes in here later. I think I'll have a surprise you'll really like."

"Make it five?"

Laughing, she slipped her hand into his and turned toward the door. "You never cease to amaze me."

He squeezed her hand in response and tugged her toward the kitchen.

He amazed her, huh? Wait until she saw what he had in mind for after dessert.

~

"Ready or not, here I come."

Aidan heard a muffled, "this isn't hide and seek," from behind the bathroom door before it creaked open and Beth stuck her head around it.

"You're wearing too many clothes for what I have in mind in here," she said, her cheeky grin in contrast to her mock frown as her gaze slid down his body. "Way too many clothes."

"Easily rectified." He whipped his T-shirt off in record time and flung it on a nearby chair, his fingers snapping the top button of his jeans undone before she reached out and stilled his hand.

"On second thoughts, I'll take care of that."

Opening the door wider she stepped aside and gestured him in with a theatrical flourish.

"What the—"

"I know it's not a guy thing but you said you'd never taken a bath so I thought now was as good a time as any for it to be your first time."

His jaw dropped as he took in the candles of all shapes and sizes strategically placed around the bathroom to cast an inviting glow, the rose petals floating on the steaming water filling the bath, and the topped up wine glasses within easy reach of the tub.

"I know it's probably not your thing but I thought—"

"It's great. Really." He cupped her cheek for a moment, impressed by the effort she'd gone to, blown away by how much thought she'd put into this. "I'm assuming you got all this stuff from under the vanity?"

"Uh-huh. I'm sure your folks won't mind."

He didn't care if they did. Right now, all he wanted to do was immerse himself in that tempting body of water, followed by the tempting body of the woman who'd done all this for him.

"So are you going to step into the bathroom or stay out there all night?"

Smiling, he let her lead him in by the hand, inhaling sharply as a delicious aroma reminiscent of freshly baked sweet rolls slammed into his senses.

"Vanilla and cinnamon bath bombs," she said, reading his mind as he breathed in several lungfuls of the heady fragrance, wondering if the scent would linger on her soft skin after they bathed together, knowing it would tempt him to taste every inch of her all night long.

He snagged his finger into the top of her skirt and tugged. "What were you saying a minute ago about wearing too many clothes?"

"Patience..."

They reached the tub and he forced himself to stand perfectly still, his arms loose by his sides as Beth stepped closer, her fingers toying with his zip while she stared up at him with a naughty glint in her eyes.

"You're killing me," he muttered, as she slid the zip down inch by inch, the rasp of the metal teeth drowning out his whoosh of air as she completed her task, slid her hands inside the waistband, and eased the denim off his hips.

"You can't rush a good bath." Her sizzling glance from beneath lowered lashes would've fried him on the spot if he wasn't already near boiling point.

Standing back, she tapped her bottom lip with her finger and stared directly at his crotch. "Hmm...still too many clothes."

However, as she reached for his cotton boxers, he grabbed her wrist. "Not so fast. Seeing as this is the first time for me, I'm a little nervous. I think I need my hand held in that tub."

Her lips curved in a slow, wicked smile. "Bet that's not all you need held."

His chuckles died as she shimmied out of her denim mini and jade halter top in a second, leaving her standing less than two feet away from him in a skimpy lace thong the exact striking green of her top.

"Last one in is a rotten pterodactyl egg," she said, peeling the lace down her long legs with the panache of someone at total ease with their body, before stepping into the bath and sinking below the waterline, ruining his view of the good stuff completely.

He shucked his boxers in record time and joined her in the bath, his sharp intake of breath having little to do with the hot water temperature and everything to do with Beth sitting up to make room for him and her nipples skimming the surface of the water.

"Turn around," he commanded, eager to feel her flush against him, to fill his hands with her.

"Jeez, you're bossy."

However, she did exactly as she was told, settling her back against his chest and resting her head on his shoulder as they both lay back and let the soothing water overlap them.

"Comfortable?"

"Very," she murmured, wriggling her butt against his erection to prove it.

"Good. I've heard it's important to relax while having a good soak."

He cupped her breasts as he spoke, savoring their weight in his palms, lightly pinching the nipples until they jutted.

She moaned, her head lolling back further as he slid his hands down her stomach in a long, slow caress until he slid a finger between her slick folds.

"Relaxed yet?"

"Getting there." She gasped, her voice barely audible as her pelvis thrust upward in reaction to the leisurely exploration of his fingers.

Empowered by her soft mewling sounds, he grazed her clitoris repeatedly, touching her with the lightest of pressure, savoring the thrill of how much he turned her on.

"Aidan..."

Her escalating pants encouraged him to pick up the tempo and in a heartbeat she stiffened and cried out, her head digging into his shoulder as her body arched out of the water before sinking below the surface on a sigh.

"I'm really getting the hang of this bath caper," he murmured, brushing a lingering kiss across her mouth, knowing he'd never be able to step into this room again without remembering the electrifying sounds she made as she came.

"This bath was supposed to be all about you." She stared at him with wonder in her eyes, large, limpid, moss-green pools he could lose himself in forever.

"You don't think I'm enjoying it?" He gave a little upthrust of his hips, leaving her in little doubt as to exactly how much he was enjoying it.

In response, she sat upright and flipped around, straddling him before he could blink.

Bracing her hands on his shoulders, she leaned forward until her nipples brushed his chest, her breath the barest whisper against his cheek. "I want you."

With blood pounding through his veins and every cell in his body screaming for release, he forced himself to lean back and intertwine his fingers behind his head, a small part of him wanting to prolong the pleasure, vindicated by the hungry glint in her eyes.

His slow smile was designed to tease. "Then take me. I'm all yours."

Beth's breath caught as Aidan's erection nudged her

entrance and she cursed, darting a frantic glance around in the hope a condom would miraculously appear out of thin air.

"Ah..." He held onto her tight as he surged out of the water. "I think what you're after is in the bedroom?"

"Actually, it's right here." Her hand zeroed in on his erection as she slid down his body to stand dripping on the bathmat. "But you're right, the bedroom is a great idea considering what I'd like to do with this."

She gave him a gentle squeeze and he groaned, his tortured expression leaving her in little doubt he couldn't hold out much longer.

"You like?" Her voice came out a purr and he growled in response, grabbing the nearest towel and enveloping both their bodies, creating an intimate cocoon of hot flesh and barely restrained desire.

"You shouldn't tease a man when he's on the brink," he murmured, backing her toward the bed when she didn't ease up her grip.

"Who said I'm teasing?"

Chuckling, he whipped off the towel as they tumbled onto the king size bed, its cushiony softness molding around their heated bodies.

So he didn't have satin sheets? It didn't matter considering the star of Beth's every recent fantasy was propped above her, staring at her like she was one of his prized artefacts.

"I'm usually a patient man but I've got to tell you right now I'm feeling mighty impatient."

Beth loved the way his eyes lit up when he looked at her, loved the sexy smile playing about his mouth.

Loved?

Stunned by the depth of feeling Aidan created within

her, she quickly amended her thoughts to *liking* everything about him.

Love didn't enter the equation.

Not for her.

"We've got all night to take it slow." She reached up to pull his head down toward her. "Right now, I feel the need for speed."

"You're amazing," he whispered against the side of her mouth a second before his lips closed over hers in a heart-stopping kiss that left her panting when he momentarily broke contact to slide the top drawer of the bedside table open, grapple with a condom, and sheath himself before picking up where he'd left off.

Her body turned to liquid heat as his hands smoothed over her body, exploring every dip, caressing every curve, while kissing her the entire time, deep, hungry, passionate kisses that wiped her mind of all rational thought bar one: how much she wanted—needed—him inside her this very minute.

As if reading her mind he parted her legs with gentle pressure from his thighs and eased into her, inch by exquisite inch, his tongue mimicking exactly what he'd be doing to her for as long as she could hold out.

But she didn't want this time to be slow. She wanted hard and fast, and wrapping her ankles around his butt she surged upward, taking him into the hilt, expanding around him, throbbing with need.

With a loud groan he gave up the last vestige of restraint and started to move, faster, harder, pounding into her as her body strained to meet him thrust for thrust.

Tension coiled within her, grew and spread, driving her wild with the mind-numbing pleasure of it all. She teetered on the verge for a heart-stopping second before plunging over the other side into orgasmic oblivion, her cries joining his as he skyrocketed to the moon and back right alongside her.

Sinking back into the bed, she welcomed his weight as he lay on top of her, cuddling her close.

They didn't speak.

They didn't need to, two people in perfect sync.

Oh yeah, she definitely *liked* a lot of things about Aidan.

As long as she didn't go getting any crazy ideas about that other L word, she could handle liking him just fine.

CHAPTER TEN

Beth usually had no problems with the morning-after scenario. Besides, they'd already faced that particular situation twenty-four hours earlier.

However, as she padded down the hallway toward the kitchen, following the aromatic trail of sizzling bacon, she knew this was no ordinary morning-after.

This was the morning-after the night before she realized she was in way over her head.

Aidan didn't do flings, as he'd clearly demonstrated with every touch, every intimate smile, every whispered endearment all night.

Lana had been right. Aidan was a stayer. Leaving Beth no other option but to establish some much needed distance between them.

"Yeah, Dad, the museum's fine, running like clockwork."

She paused in the doorway, swallowing the lump in her throat at the sight of him wearing nothing but soft cotton boxers the same dove-grey shade as his eyes, cradling a cell between his ear and shoulder while deftly flipping bacon with the other hand.

His back muscles rippled with every movement of his arm, his long bare legs sending an instant flush of heat through her as she remembered how they'd felt entwined with hers as he'd slid into her last night...several times...

The sound of his low, harried voice brought her back to the present and she took a step toward the doorway as he spoke.

"I don't know what my plans are at this stage."

She halted in her tracks, knowing she should make her presence known but holding back, surprised by his exasperated tone.

"Look, when I know what I'm doing I'll let you know. But for now, don't worry, I'm staying in Melbourne. I've met someone and she's a keeper."

Her blood chilled and she gripped the doorjamb for support as her knees threatened to buckle.

She wasn't a keeper.

How could she be, when she couldn't give a guy like Aidan what he wanted—a real relationship?

"You just take it easy, I've got a handle on things down here. I'll talk to you soon."

She tried to back away from the doorway before he caught sight of her but she was a fraction late as he turned to grab a plate from the island bench.

"Hey, there you are. Hungry?"

The tenderness in his eyes reached out and beckoned, warm and secure, openly accepting of her.

But she couldn't do this. Couldn't do it to herself or to him.

Faking a smile, she bounced into the room rather than

slinking out the front door and never returning as she wanted to do. "Starving. Hope the bacon's crispy."

"I remember how you liked it from yesterday morning."

He slid a plate piled high with poached eggs—yokes runny, just perfect—crispy bacon, and hash browns toward her, accompanied by a lingering kiss that made her stiffen.

"What's wrong?"

"Nothing," she said, far too quickly as she concentrated on dissecting her food with a knife and fork, wishing they didn't have to have this conversation, knowing it was inevitable.

"Beth, look at me."

Sighing, she placed the cutlery neatly together in the center of her plate, her appetite vanishing when she raised her gaze to meet his.

"Was it something about last night? Because if it was—"

"This isn't about something you did." She dashed a hand across her eyes, shocked by the sudden sting. She never cried, just like she never fell for any of the guys she dated.

Well, well, looked like today was a day for firsts.

"Then what? I don't get it." He wiped his hands on the dishcloth before flinging it on the island bench and stepping around it, coming to an abrupt halt when she shrank away from him, hands held up to ward him off. "What the hell is going on here?"

She lowered her arms nd she shook her head, wishing there was an easy way to say this, all too aware there wasn't.

"This isn't what I want."

A frown creased his brow, confusion clouding his face. "What, breakfast?"

"You know what I'm talking about." She slid off the stool and headed toward the door, needing some distance between them to deliver her walk-out speech. "This fling we have going on is getting a bit serious."

Realization dawned in his eyes as bewilderment gave way to concern. "But we haven't discussed a relationship."

"Yet."

Shaking his head, he braced against the bench top with his arms and her traitorous body gave a lurch at the way his pecs stood out, the same way they had when he'd been propped over her last night, satisfying her every desire.

"Okay, so you're right. I do want to talk about us and where we're going. In fact, I wanted to do it last night but we got sidetracked."

His eyes darkened to stormy at the memory of what they'd shared, of how amazing it had been and she blinked, needing to dispel the intimate spell that had descended on them the minute he mentioned last night.

Ignoring the intense regret stabbing her conscience, she squared her shoulders and looked him straight in the eye. "But that's just it. We're not going anywhere. There is no us."

The tiny scar above his right eye twitched, a similar action she'd seen several times when he'd been stressed at work.

"Nice try, but I'm not buying it. You can't fake what we have."

"And what's that? A bit of chemistry?"

His jaw clenched, his biceps bulging further as he gripped the bench top tighter. "There's more to it than a simple attraction between us and you know it."

Determined to put an end to this before the sting behind her eyes turned into a waterfall, she shrugged as if she didn't give a damn. "What I know is we don't have a hope of sustaining a relationship or whatever it is you think we might have going here. It would never work."

"Coward." He pushed off the bench top and crossed the kitchen in two seconds flat to take hold of her upper arms, his touch wreaking as much havoc as his words. "How can you say we wouldn't work if you're too damn chicken to try?"

Beth couldn't think, couldn't breathe, with his hands touching her, even in an innocuous way. Her skin prickled beneath his hands, wanting more, needing more, and she struggled to break free only to have him hold on tighter.

"You're not walking out of here until we settle this," he said, his grim expression at odds with the hurt in his eyes.

Swallowing the emotion lodged firmly in her throat, she knew there was only one way to end this. She had to hurt him badly enough for him to let her go.

"Fine. You want to settle this?" She tilted her chin up, her heart sinking at the flicker of hope in his unwavering stare. "I said we wouldn't work to lighten the blow. What I really meant was, I could never go for a guy like you, a desk jockey who's content to give up his dream to settle for second best."

She wriggled in his arms, hating what she had to do, hating the pain in his eyes, but most of all, hating herself for not having the guts to shake off every inbuilt self-preservation mechanism that stopped her from taking a risk on a fantastic guy like him.

"And that's what the museum is to you, second best. I see it when you drag your ass in there every morning. I see it every time you have to resolve some pissy little problem. Your eyes light up with fire when you check out some of those old exhibits in a way they never have in a staff meeting."

Or when they checked out her, but she couldn't go there, couldn't think about it now. Not when she was so close to achieving what she'd set out to do. Anger warred with shock in his incredible grey eyes so she took advantage of his surprise and shrugged off his hands.

"I'm living my life the way I want to, Aidan. Can you say the same?"

She had no intention of waiting around for his answer, but as she swiveled toward the door he made a strange, almost strangled sound that had her turning back.

"You're wrong about me," he said, a hint of steel underlying his grim pronouncement, the tiny scar near his eyebrow giving an infinitesimal flicker as he frowned.

"Am I?"

She forced her feet to move, determined to ignore the pain in her chest, the deep seated ache that belied every word she'd uttered, the soul-deep certainty that for once in her life she should've taken a chance on love.

~

AIDAN DID what he'd always done when he needed to blow off steam: he dug.

After grabbing an old shovel of his dad's, he headed into the backyard and stabbed at the soil in the overgrown veggie patch, enjoying the bite of steel in his instep as he pushed down on the shovel, relishing the twinge in his back as he hoisted a monstrous clump of dirt and flung it as far as he could.

He repeated the action over and over, the mindless repetition soothing as always. With every clump he overturned, his tension dissipated, until he leaned forward on the shovel and wiped his brow, sweat pouring off him, feeling lighter than he had in months.

He should've been angry after Beth's tirade. Hell, he should've been downright fuming after everything she'd said. Instead, with the sun beating down on him and his muscles aching like they hadn't in ages, all he could think was how right she'd been.

He hadn't been truly happy since he'd taken over as CEO at the museum and he missed the hands-on digging and discovery work more than he'd thought possible.

He *was* going through the motions on a daily basis, trying to fool himself into liking the job and for what? Another futile attempt at getting his dad's approval? He should know better by now.

His cell rang and he swiped his hands down the side of his jeans before fishing it out of his pocket. His heart sank as he saw the museum's number flash up on the screen.

He'd barely answered when a female voice said, "Aidan, it's Dorothy MacPherson here, from the museum."

Surprised a volunteer would be calling him, he stabbed the shovel into the dirt and propped a foot on it. "What can I do for you?"

"I've got a bit of a problem. A tour company in the Northern Territory just called, requesting up front payment for the extra four wheel drive vehicle your father has booked. And there's no one here to authorize it, so I don't know what to do. They sounded pretty uptight and said it was urgent so—"

"There must be some mistake. My father's not in the Northern Territory, he's taking indefinite sick leave in Queensland."

Dorothy paused before clearing her throat with a

nervous little cough. "Um, the tour company faxed through an invoice and it has a lot of other items on it. When I asked to speak to your father, they said he was searching some caves in Kakadu."

Aidan froze. Disappointment roiled in his gut, thick and heavy, as he gripped the handle of the shovel so tightly tiny splinters of wood drove into the newly formed calluses on his palm. He barely registered the sting. It had nothing on the pain and disillusionment exploding through him, the agony of finally waking up and facing the truth.

His father had manipulated him, again.

Abe wasn't so ill he needed to rest interstate. Oh no, he was off chasing artefacts in the outback while his son was chained to a desk, doing exactly what dear old dad wanted.

Damn, he'd been a fool.

He'd thought the old man had changed, had reached out to him in an effort to bridge the yawning gap between them.

He'd thought wrong.

Frustrated to the point of wanting to snap the shovel in two, he threw it away while gripping his cell to his ear with the other.

"Don't worry about the invoice, Dorothy. I'll come in and take care of it."

The sharp intake of breath on the other end of the line alerted him to the fact that some of the bitterness flooding him must've spilled over into his voice and he took a calming breath.

"And thanks for contacting me. You did the right thing."

"Okay, Mr. Voss. Bye."

He slid his cell into his pocket, picked up the shovel and moved over to the empty flower beds. He had a lot of digging to do to ease the animosity making him want to jump on a plane this instant, find his father, and ram the truth down his lying throat.

At least he now knew what he had to do.

And when it was done, let Beth tell him he wasn't the right guy for her.

∼

BETH TRUDGED INTO THE MUSEUM, her feet dragging.

She was *so* over this.

The sooner Lana threw away her crutches and took over the tours, the better. In the meantime, Beth would suck it up and try not to cringe over the harsh stuff she'd said to Aidan because she was too immature to handle the truth: that for the first time in her life, she wanted more than a fling.

His wounded expression when she'd told him that whopping great lie—that she could never go for a guy like him—played on repeat in her mind, no matter how hard she tried to forget it. She could go for him all right. She already had and, like the finest *Moretti's* chocolate, one taste had her addicted.

"Hey Beth, wait up."

Sighing, she fixed her usual 'all's right with the world' smile on her face, something she'd been doing her entire life, and turned to Dorothy.

"Hi Dot..." the rest of her greeting died on her lips as she took in the young woman's new layered haircut with highlights falling around her face in soft waves, colored contact lens, figure-enhancing bottle green skirt suit, and snappy black patent ballet flats.

"Some transformation, huh?" Dot flicked her hair over her shoulder and winked.

"You look fantastic." At least some good had come out of her work here.

"All thanks to you." Dot did a little pirouette, her confident smile growing by the minute. "You may not know a lot about the museum but you're a whiz with fashion."

"You know I'm not really qualified to take tours, don't you?"

Dot shrugged. "All I know is I'm surprised you got the job here when you seem a bit out of the loop?"

She laughed at Dot's diplomacy. "You mean I stink, don't you?"

"Well, when you put it that way..." Dot joined in her laughter and she beckoned her over to a secluded spot near the entrance so she could explain why she made such a lousy tour guide. She'd bonded with Dot during the makeover sessions and knew she could trust her.

"My cousin Lana Walker is the new head curator. She got the job but suffered a hairline fracture of her ankle before she could start. I needed a job, so she got me an interview with Abraham Voss and he said I could fill in as tour guide until Lana's back on her feet."

Dot reached out and squeezed her arm and, for the second time in as many hours, Beth blinked back inexplicable tears. "Considering your lack of knowledge, you've done great."

She swallowed the unexpected lump of emotion in her throat. Dot's kindness was really getting to her. "If you think I'm great, wait until you meet Lana. She's so brainy she'll blow you away."

"I can't wait to meet her. We should have loads in common."

Glancing at Dot's trendy suit and subtle make up, Beth doubted it.

"It'll be great for Lana to have a friend when she eventually gets here. Maybe we can all go for a drink before she starts?" With the added bonus of providing a distraction from her screw-up with the boss. "There's a new vodka ice bar I've been dying to try."

Dot's eyes lit up. "Sounds great."

"Okay, leave it with me and I'll tee it up. Now, I must dash. Tours to take, exhibits to be clueless about."

Dot chuckled and waved her off, while Beth turned toward the huge front doors.

She could do this.

After all, it wasn't the first time she'd had to pretend all was right with the world when it wasn't.

∾

AIDAN GLANCED AROUND HIS OFFICE, not in the least surprised it didn't look any different from when he'd first taken on the job. His meager belongings filled a single cardboard box, which proved how he hadn't settled in as much as he'd fooled himself into thinking.

He'd finally made the right decision for all of them, and if Abe didn't agree, tough.

Aidan was done trying to do the right thing in an effort to impress Abe, and done trying to get his father's attention no matter what the cost.

As if on cue, his cell rang and he glanced at the caller, relieved his dad had called back and he could soon put all this behind him.

He took a steadying breath and answered. "Thanks for getting back to me so quickly."

"Everything all right with the museum? Your message sounded serious."

Aidan shook his head. Typical Abraham Voss. He could be calling for any number of personal reasons but the first thing dear old dad thought about was his precious museum.

"Everything's fine here. Though I wanted to let you know I've resigned. I'll give you two weeks to find a replacement, then I'm out of here. Though I'm sure you could always tear yourself away from Kakadu and step up if you're desperate."

Abe's harsh intake of breath didn't surprise him, nor did the explosive expletive. "What brought all this on?"

Aidan propped against the desk, his heart heavy. Even now, his father couldn't apologize for feeding him a load of bull about recuperating in Queensland, when in fact he'd been jerking his strings, making him dance to his tune, like he always tried to do.

Time to come clean...about everything.

"The only reason I took this job was to please you, Dad. It's pretty much why I became an archaeologist, why I've done a lot of things in my life. It's been the only way to get your attention half the time."

Another muttered expletive from Abe, but still no apology.

"This is ludicrous. Your mother and I have always cared about you."

"Yeah, but caring didn't extend to you being there for my first day at school, or the time I made school captain, or the time I was dux at uni. And it sure as hell doesn't extend to you being upfront with me about why you want me working here."

That hurt most of all; after all this time, his father still couldn't be honest with him. He treated him like a subordinate, someone to be kept in the dark and fed on BS.

Not anymore.

"Where's all this coming from?" As expected, his father's audible confusion showed Abe didn't have a clue.

"Honestly? I should've said this a long time ago. Guess I still hoped you'd change, but I'm done being your stooge. Not after this stunt you pulled."

"Look, Son, I just wanted to give you a feel for the job, to see if you liked it before I made any decisions." To his surprise, Abe sounded distressed rather than the angry or defensive as he'd expected.

"That's bull." Running a hand over his face, he took a steadying breath, knowing he had to stay calm to get his point across. It was now or never. If Abe didn't get it now, he never would. "You manipulated me, Dad, just like you always have. You wanted me to do exactly what you wanted so you pulled the sick card, knowing I wouldn't say no. Want to know the stupid part? I thought you needed me for once, that you might actually care enough to reach out. But I was wrong. You used me. You put your needs first as always."

"Well, then." Abe exhaled and silence reigned for a few seconds before he cleared his throat like he had a million frogs stuck in it. "You're right, I want you to take over as CEO permanently but I knew you wouldn't go for it if I asked, so I wanted to give you a little taste of it, make sure you'd step up."

Abe's admission should've eased the bitterness. It didn't. It merely served to reinforce the huge emotional gap between them.

"So you played up your heart problems?"

Abe sighed, sounding wearier than he ever had. "My blood pressure is under control with medication and I haven't had an angina attack in a while. Yes, I had to take a break on doctor's orders but not for this long. That was me hoping you'd like the top job enough to stay."

"You manipulated me."

This time, he spoke without rancor. A flat statement that no amount of ranting or raving or emotion could change.

"Yes, I did. I was grooming you and this was the only way I thought to get you to do it."

No apology, no back down. But then, what did Aidan expect? Selfish people couldn't see what they did was wrong. The end always justified the means.

"I can't change your mind?"

Appalled by his father's gall, Aidan said, "No. And unlike you, I have a conscience and don't only think of myself, so like I said, I'll give you a few weeks to find a replacement but after that I'm out of here."

He could've sworn he heart a choked sound akin to a sob down the line but that couldn't be right. That would mean his dad cared and Abe didn't. Not by a long shot.

"You didn't really become an archaeologist to get my attention, did you?"

A good question, something Aidan had pondered at length over the last twenty-four hours.

"Actually, my career choice wasn't all about you. I guess you and mum instilled your love of old stuff into me from a young age, and hanging around all those dig sites spurred me on. That's the only time you ever paid me real attention, when I found something."

Another sharp intake of breath let out on a slow hiss, before Abe said, "I'm sorry, Son. I had no idea."

And just like that, some of Aidan's residual animosity dissolved. Ironic, considering he'd spent a lifetime carrying around this baggage and all it took was a simple apology to lift the weight from his shoulders.

"That's the first time you've ever apologized for anything."

"I know, and I'm sorry about that too." Abe paused and Aidan could imagine his dad's expression—brow furrowed, deep grooves bracketing his mouth—what he'd always labelled his 'thinking' face. "I'll be flying back once I wrap things up here. Can we have a man to man chat as soon as I get back to Melbourne?"

"I probably won't be around. Maybe next time I'm in town?"

"When will that be?"

"No idea at this stage."

It all depended on Beth and whether she went for his plan or not.

"Stay in touch, won't you, son?"

He'd never heard his father sound so humble and it gave him hope that maybe they could salvage something from their relationship after all.

"Uh-huh."

Aidan almost disconnected when his dad rushed in. "Son, your mother and I are proud of you, always have been."

It was the closest Aidan would get to a declaration of love and for now, it had to be enough. He knew Abe was a thinker, someone who would ponder this conversation at length before drawing his own conclusions.

"Thanks, Dad, bye."

After sliding his cell into his jacket pocket, he took one last look around the office, picked up his box, and headed for the door.

Time for this staid professor to start living again.

CHAPTER
ELEVEN

Beth double checked the address on the fancy embossed card, looked up at the swank city gallery, and back at the card.

This couldn't be the right place.

She'd been invited to scope out a possible home for her next collection, and considering it would take at least six months for the lease to come through on her own space, she'd been interested. The weird thing was, it looked like this gallery wasn't only considering her next collection, as every piece she'd made for her last collection already took pride of place here.

The front windows were filled with twisted metal shrubs, flowers, and garden gnomes, her interpretation of the heritage gardens around Melbourne, and some of her best work.

Cupping her hands against the glass, she pressed her face between them, so shocked she stumbled back.

It wasn't just the front windows housing her work. The whole damn gallery was filled with it, the metal pieces at odds with a heap of old masks and pottery pieces and ceramics. Not to mention her Sydney Opera House taking pride of place on a raised dais in the middle of the room.

"What the..." She trailed off as she stepped inside the gallery, her mouth dropping open as Aidan popped up from behind the glass and chrome counter, looking more relaxed than she'd ever seen him.

"What are you doing here?"

He didn't respond immediately, his charismatic smile sending her belly into a free fall she had no hope of recovering from. It had always been like this, from the first minute she met him and, despite the wedge she'd deliberately driven between them, it looked like her reaction to the sexy CEO hadn't waned at all.

"Well? What's this all about?"

He shrugged, his shoulders impossibly broad in black cashmere as he came around from behind the counter to stand in front of her. "This is our place."

"Our place?"

She shook her head, feeling like she'd stepped into a time warp or some weird alternate universe where everyone knew what was going on but her.

"I want a place to show-case our work so I've leased this space, bought the unsold pieces from your last collection, trumped the top bidder for the fundraiser piece, and added some of my own stuff. I'm confident we can keep the place stocked with your work and my new finds."

She hated the traitorous leap of hope her heart gave. "That's going to be difficult, finding stuff from behind a desk, isn't it?"

He tipped her chin up, his smile patient. "I quit."

Brushing away his hand—she couldn't think with the havoc his touch wrought on her body—she said, "Hope it wasn't on my account."

"Actually, this has everything to do with you."

She took a step back at the intent in his eyes. He looked way too confident, too intense, too focused—on her.

"You were right. Being stuck behind a desk isn't me."

"So you choose to run a gallery instead? Wow, why don't you live a little?" Her sarcasm fell on deaf ears as his smile broadened.

"I'm going back to what I love best, getting my hands dirty in the thick of a dig."

Feeling like a prized dummy for jumping to conclusions, and for giving him grief when he didn't deserve it, she mumbled, "I'm happy for you."

Stepping into her personal space, he ran a hand lightly up her arm. "Aren't you going to ask me what this has to do with you?"

"No."

She bit down on her bottom lip to keep from crying out as his hand slipped into hers, his thumb slowly caressing her palm in small circles.

"Fine, I'll tell you anyway. You said you wouldn't go for a guy like me? Well, I'm going to prove you wrong. Hopefully, this place is the first step in showing you that."

"You think by mingling the stuff we do for a living I'll change my mind?"

She shook her head, hating how impressed she was by the effort he'd gone to, how tempted she was to renege on her previous stance.

But she couldn't. Even if he'd made a career choice for the better, it didn't mean he'd stop pushing her for more emotional commitment if they picked up where they left off.

"This place doesn't change a thing."

His cool expression faltered for the first time since she'd

arrived, the scar above his right eye twitching ever so slightly. "You're scared."

"Of what? You?" She forced a laugh and wrenched her hand out of his, needing space before she leaned into him and wiped the worry off his face with a kiss she so desperately wanted to deliver.

"Of us. Of a relationship. Of how damn good we could be together given half a chance."

Every tiny arrow of truth he shot at her found its mark, embedding in her heart and rendering her speechless with the pain of it.

Balling her hands, she tugged her bag in front of her, knowing it would prove useless as shield if he touched her again.

"This is irrelevant. You're going away and I'm not the sit at home and knit type while I wait for you to drop in whenever you're in the neighborhood."

"But you wouldn't have to wait at home for me." Thrusting a hand into his back pocket, he pulled out a slimline black folder and handed it to her. "Here. This should clear up a few more of your preconceptions."

Flipping open the folder, she stared at the airline ticket, destination Rio de Janeiro, more confused than ever when she spied her name in the 'passenger' box.

Her gaze flew to his, hating the crazy out of control feeling swamping her while his calm demeanor remained unruffled. "What's this supposed to mean?"

"We're alike, you and me. We're adventurers. We like to live each day as it comes. We're spontaneous. I'm all the things you are even if you don't want to believe it for fear of getting too close."

Damn, he was good. He knew exactly how she was feeling, how she'd felt from the start. By trying to convince herself they were nothing alike, she could hold him at bay.

But deep down she'd known the truth all along.

She loved his adventurous side.

She loved his spontaneity

She loved—no, she couldn't—liked him.

"Want some proof? I want you to travel with me to South America. I want you to give us a chance. I want a relationship with you. Quite simply, I want it all."

Before she could move he captured her face between his hands and crushed his mouth to hers, the kiss a startling combination of heat, passion and desperation, a soul-drugging kiss designed to bewitch, bother and bewilder.

And she was definitely all three, her mind shutting down the instant he deepened the kiss, his tongue eagerly searching out hers, his lips softening, his hands leaving her face to slide down her torso and cup her butt, drawing her firmly against him.

She knew this would have to stop, would have to be the last kiss they ever shared, so she gave herself over to the bliss of the moment, taking as well as giving, savoring every sigh, every caress, imprinting it on her brain to be resurrected at will.

"Say yes," he whispered, his thumbs brushing the corners of her mouth, his incredible slate eyes beseeching her to agree.

For one heart-rending, hope-filled moment, Beth wanted to throw caution to the wind and say yes.

She wanted to fling every reservation she'd ever had about relationships out the window and go for it.

But she couldn't, for while her heart was screaming 'yes, yes, yes', her head resurrected memories of her father and how he'd fallen apart when her mom died, how he'd never recovered, how loving and losing could be devastating for the rest of one's days.

She never let anyone get too close because she didn't want to feel that kind of soul-deep pain. Nobody was worth it. She'd made sure of it her entire life and she couldn't change now, even for the most spectacular man she'd ever met.

"I can't." She turned away and dashed a hand across her eyes, simultaneously dashing any faint hope they might've had.

Aidan didn't reach for her again.

He didn't move, didn't speak, and she finally raised her eyes to meet his, his pain quickly masked by a puzzling perceptiveness.

"I'm sorry. I'm not cut out for a relationship." She lifted her hands in a helpless gesture before letting them fall uselessly to her sides, trying not to take gulps of air to fill her oxygen deprived lungs, to ease the pain squeezing her heart in a vice.

He studied her through narrowed eyes, his expression inscrutable. "You're the one who prompted me to take a risk, to confront my dad, to toss in my job, and you were right. I've spent a lifetime trying to get the old man's attention and it took a headstrong, talented, intelligent, beautiful woman to make me see what a senseless waste of time it was. And the funny thing? I thought you had a hell of a lot more gumption than this."

She wanted to go to him so badly her body ached. "I didn't know all that stuff about your dad."

He waved away her concern. "It's not important. What's important is you and me getting on the same page. I'm there. How about you?"

She shook her head and turned away, unable to look at him a moment longer. "Relationships aren't my thing."

She stiffened as he came up behind her and rested both hands on her shoulders, bending to murmur in her ear. "The plane ticket is yours. I leave in a week. I'll wait for you at the gate."

"Please don't."

Her whispered plea sounded pathetic in the loaded silence and, with a gentle squeeze of her shoulders and a tender, lingering kiss on the nape of her neck, he walked away.

Leaving Beth more conflicted than ever.

∼

BETH STUMBLED from the gallery in such a daze it took her a full half hour and a tram ride to Lana's house before she realized she still had the plane ticket clutched in her hand.

She thrust it into her jacket pocket where it burned a hole, a reminder of what she could have if she took a chance.

How ironic, that risk was her middle name, yet when it came to taking the ultimate gamble—with her heart—she was as yellow bellied as a snake.

"You better come in before you wear out my footpath." Lana held open her front door and it took Beth a full five seconds to absorb what was different about her cousin.

"Hey, no crutches."

Lana did a little twirl, ending in a stumble. "Great, huh? Almost as good as new."

"That's fabulous news."

That made it official: Beth's stint at the museum had finished, along with her all too brief fling with Aidan.

"I thought you'd be happier?" A tiny worry line creased Lana's brow and Beth shook her head, knowing she shouldn't have come here, but having no one else to turn to.

"I am happy for you being back on your feet, especially as you you'll be at the museum rather than me." Beth screwed up her nose. "I'm in a funk because I'm a stubborn mule."

Lana chuckled. "Is that all? For a moment I thought it was serious."

"It is serious, if you consider me being offered the world by an amazing guy and turning it down serious."

The worry line reappeared as Lana opened the door wider. "You better come in. This calls for chocolate."

"It'll take ten blocks to even begin to cure me."

"You've been bitten, I see." Lana rummaged through her pantry before plonking a family size block of nougat chocolate on the table and flicking the kettle on.

"Bitten?" Beth broke off an entire row of mouthwatering chocolate and stuffed six small blocks into her mouth at once, hoping the sugar and cocoa fix would ease her pain. It didn't.

Lana propped against a bench and grinned. "By the love bug."

"Ha, ha, you're a real riot." Beth reached for the chocolate again before pushing it away with a groan. "What am I doing? Stuffing myself until I'm sick isn't going to solve anything."

"But the endorphins will make you feel better."

Beth could think of a much better way to get her endorphins spiking and it had nothing to do with eating chocolate and everything to do with getting naked with the one guy who had rocked her world.

"So you fell in love with my boss? Nice."

"He's not your boss anymore."

Lana straightened so fast she knocked a spatula off the bench and it clattered to the floor. "What?"

"Aidan quit. He's going back to archaeology."

"But what about the museum?"

"I'm sure it's still there. After all, it ran perfectly well before he arrived on the scene, right?"

"Right." Lana nodded, her eyes round orbs behind her glasses. "Of course, I'm being silly. A guy with Aidan Voss's reputation wouldn't leave the museum in the lurch." Lana paused, her eyes widening. "Ohhh…now I get it. That's why you're upset? Because he's leaving?"

Beth shook her head. "He asked me to go with him."

"What?" Lana's screech had Beth reaching for the chocolate again. "That's the most romantic thing I've ever heard."

"Hold onto your heart, romcom queen. I turned him down."

"You *what*? But why?"

"Because he wants a relationship."

Lana frowned. "And?"

"I don't do relationships."

The kettle whistled at that moment and Lana busied herself making two hot chocolates complete with marshmallows before taking a seat at the dining table and pushing a steaming mug across to her.

"That's not what you said the night I got the job."

Beth took a sip of the hot chocolate and sighed, savouring the slide of rich chocolate across her tastebuds. "Honestly, Cuz? I don't have much recollection of what I said that night. As I recall, I was pretty wasted, celebrating *your* dream job."

Leaning forward and fixing her with the 'listen up' glare

she'd had down pat since childhood, Lana said, "You said you wanted a family of your own. Hubby, kids, the works, but you were too damned scared to let any guy get too close for fear of losing him."

"I said that?" Beth hid behind her mug, silently vowing to stay clear of celebratory Cosmopolitans no matter what the occasion.

"There's more. You offloaded about your folks, and how your mom was the love of your dad's life and how he shut down after she died and didn't have anything left to give you."

Beth cringed. "Like you didn't know. You were there the whole time, you saw it. He basically waited until we turned eighteen before pegging out.

"You don't know that."

"Yeah, I do," Beth snapped, instantly regretting her outburst when Lana flinched. "Sorry. I know you're just trying to help and I know you lost your parents too, but my dad—"

"You didn't lose both your parents. Your dad was still around."

"No, he wasn't. That's why I can't do this..." Her last words ended on a sob and she swiped a hand over her eyes, holding up her other hand to stop Lana from hugging her.

"It was like he was dead to me. He didn't care about me once he lost Mom. I didn't exist anymore, he loved her that much, and I could never do that to another person. I don't want to ever love that much so I shut down when I lose them. It's masochistic."

"It's life," Lana said softly, her hand resting gently on Beth's shoulder. "Aren't you the one who's always raving on about living life to the fullest, about making the most of every minute? Well, from where I'm standing, looks to me like you're not living by your own motto. How is shutting yourself off from this amazing opportunity with a guy you really like living life to the fullest?"

"I don't like him, that's the problem."

"Huh?"

"I love him."

Beth's admission came out on a sigh, a heartfelt, soul deep truth ripped from within. She'd suspected it for a while, probably from the first time he'd called her Fancy Feet, but she'd done her damnedest to ignore the truth, or sugar-coat it in terms like fling.

However, whichever way she looked at it, she was in love with Aidan, every impressive, delicious, inch of him.

"So let me get this straight," Lana said. "You love him but don't want to have the time of your life because you might lose him one day?"

I love him.

Those three little words echoed through Beth's mind, her heart, reaching down to her soul and making her ache with the joy of it.

She loved a charming, warm, sexy guy who was offering her the world...and she'd said no.

Was she nuts? Maybe she should take a chance?

Her heart clenched at the thought, a lifetime of being cautious shadowing her emotions, whispering 'it's not worth the pain'.

But she was in pain now, a constant deep-seated ache she couldn't shake no matter how much she tried to convince herself she'd made the right decision.

She loved Aidan.

It all came back to that.

Did she have the guts to confront her fear, embrace it, and take a chance on a once in a lifetime kind of love?

"Yes, I love him and no, I don't want to acknowledge it for fear of losing him one day. Sounds a bit silly when you put it like that."

Lana's gaze filled with compassion. "It's not silly, it's how you feel. But you're the ultimate risk taker. I just don't want to see you cheated out of happiness when this could be the best risk you ever take."

"As you've always told me, risk *is* my middle name," Beth muttered, a small flame of hope quickly fanned by excitement and anticipation and a wealth of possibilities, growing to a raging inferno of optimism in a second.

She could do this.

What was worse? Not taking a chance and missing out on months, maybe years of happiness with the guy she loved, or losing him one day in the future after living life to the fullest with him by her side?

"So does that mean—"

"It means you're the best cuz in the whole world." Beth leaped from her chair and flung herself at Lana, squeezing her in a bear hug until they both laughed. "Now, if you don't mind, I have some serious thinking to do."

She left Lana shaking her head, a serene smile on her face, and raced out the door, the plane ticket making comforting crinkling noises in her back pocket with every step.

She may have doubt demons dogging her but it was time to face her fears.

She just hoped it wasn't too late.

CHAPTER
TWELVE

Aidan scanned the dwindling crowd at the boarding gate, his heart sinking with every passing minute. Beth hadn't come.

He'd given her space, he'd given her his love, and she hadn't wanted any of it.

Hoisting his duffel onto his shoulder, he handed over his boarding pass, scrounging up a polite smile for the hostess who gave him an appreciative once-over. He might've been interested, if Beth hadn't branded his heart.

Damn it, was he ever going to get over her?

She'd blown into his world like a dervish, a bright, sparkly, effervescent breath of fresh air that made him feel like he could take on Mount Everest and conquer it with one hand tied behind his back.

She'd made him feel alive and filled all those tiny holes in his heart he'd barely acknowledged existed.

He didn't need to do anything to grab her attention, she'd given it unreservedly from the moment she bowled up to him with those bizarre feathery black shoes.

He loved her.

And it was over.

Every step down the long causeway was a step further away from her, a step toward closure.

He had his job.

He had his old life back.

And it wasn't enough.

Hating the ache in his chest, he nodded at the hostess at the door of the plane, ready to take his seat, plug his ears with headphones and drown out the world.

"Excuse me, Sir."

"Yes?"

What now? The plane had engine trouble? His seat was next to a faulty exit door?

"You've been upgraded to first class. If you'll follow me?"

Managing a wry smile at the twist of good luck after so much bad, he turned left and followed the hostess.

"I believe you're seated in 1A. Enjoy your flight."

"Thank you..." His jaw dropped as he registered the wide, leather seat next to him was taken—by the last person he expected to see.

"Hey there, Professor. Thought you might like some company on a long haul flight?"

He sank into the chair, the duffel sliding off his shoulder and plopping at his feet, at a loss for words as he stared at Beth and wondered if she was a by-product of his wishful thinking.

"This is a surprise," he finally managed to say, trying not to stare at her funky striped midriff top showing a tantalizing glimpse of cleavage and her bright orange flip skirt ending half way up her smooth thighs.

*Those legs...*he'd caressed those legs, kissed them, nibbled them, had them hold him in a vice-like grip, had explored every gorgeous inch of them, and he clenched his hands into fists to stop from reaching out and touching her.

"Yeah, well, I came into a lot of money because some crazy, spontaneous, sexy guy bought all the unsold pieces from my last collection, and seeing as I love to do spur of the moment things I thought I'd blow a major part of my earnings on a first class upgrade."

While her mouth curved into its signature sassy smile, uncertainty flickered in her beautiful green eyes.

Despite her bravado in showing up here like this, the woman he loved was nervous. And she had no need to be. She'd taken this gigantic step in following him to the ends of the earth and he would never let her down.

"I'm glad you're here."

Her mouth drooped in disappointment and he cursed, grabbing her hand to anchor himself, his thoughts.

"That didn't come out right. Guess I'm so blown away by you being here I can't think straight let alone put into words what I'm feeling."

"Then let me." She leaned forward and brushed her lips over his, a gentle, sensual kiss that had heat searing his body from head to foot and scorching the bits in between.

He needed little encouragement to deepen the kiss and as she grabbed at the front of his shirt, bunching it in her fists and dragging him closer, he lost it, crushing her close, tasting her, caressing her, unable to get enough. Never enough.

The sound of a discreet little cough penetrated his lust-hazed mind and he pulled back reluctantly, raising his gaze to meet the hostess's rather bland one, like she'd seen it all before.

"Champagne?"

Beth laughed, a joyous sound that made his heart sing, not in the least embarrassed as she reached across him. "Love one, thanks. Professor?"

"Thank you," he said, noting the curiosity in the hostess's eyes as her gaze flicked between them, probably wondering if he was a professor whisking a student off for some loving in South America.

"She thinks we're having an affair." Beth smirked at him from behind her flute, her green eyes sparkling.

"Well, she's mistaken. We're in a relationship."

"Yes, we are."

She held his gaze and he sighed in relief. Whatever funk she'd got into over the two of them being involved, she was over it, thank goodness.

As if sensing the direction of his thoughts, she said, "I owe you an explanation."

"You don't owe me anything."

He brushed his knuckles along her cheek, loving it when she rested against him for a moment before straightening.

"Actually, I do. You've been incredibly patient and I've behaved like a brat. I want us to start afresh and to do that you have to know what you're getting into with me, okay?"

"Okay, shoot."

Draining the rest of her champagne, she placed the flute on the console rest before laying a reassuring hand on his leg. "I've never been involved in a relationship before."

"Ever?"

She shook her head, strawberry blonde hair cascading around her shoulders like the finest gold shot with threads of ruby. "It's all a bit Freudian, actually. My parents had the perfect relationship. You know, the real soul-mate thing and as a kid I wanted something exactly like it, but that all changed when Mom died."

"Why?" He laid his hand on top of hers, hoping his soothing touch was all the incentive she needed to keep going no matter how painful.

"She was the love of my dad's life. He shut down emotionally when he lost her. Sure, he provided for me and Lana, but that was about it. For me, it felt like I grew up without both my parents, that's how withdrawn he was."

"I'm sorry."

Beth raised her gaze from where she'd been focused on their joined hands, admiring the strength in Aidan's and how perfect hers fit in it.

"I am too. Everything I've done since he died, how I've lived my life, the choices I've made, were all shaped by him. Or not wanting to be like him, to be precise."

"But you're nothing like your dad. You're bright and bubbly and live life on full throttle."

"Yeah, but somehow the 'life's short, play hard' motto didn't work when I met you."

"Why?"

He frowned and she reached up to smooth it away. "Because I was terrified of how you made me feel, of how I would feel if I fell for you and lost you."

"That's not going to happen." He captured her hand as it left his brow and drew it toward his mouth where he placed a slow, lingering kiss on her palm.

"There aren't any guarantees. You could fall down one of those giant big holes you dig while searching for some relic. You could get crushed by an ancient ruin tumbling on your head. You could—"

"Fall even harder than I already have," he murmured,

silencing her with the type of kiss she could only dream about.

"Fall?"

"In love with you."

Her breath caught as the warmth of his smile reflected in his eyes, bathing her in the reassurance she so badly needed.

"I love you too." She cupped his face in her hands and eyeballed him, beseeching him to understand what it meant for her to verbalize her feelings out loud. "And if you're willing to take a risk on an extroverted, fun-loving, metal sculptor with a shoe fetish, I'm all yours."

"No risk."

He captured her hands and slowly slid them down his torso until they rested over his heart, the steady beat another reminder of how good this guy was for her.

He would stabilize her, she would pep him up.

He would show her the world, she would show him a million different ways to enjoy it.

Yin and Yang.

Two perfect halves making a whole.

"No risk at all," he said, his gravelly tone sending a shiver of longing through her. "We're a sure thing."

"Too right," she said, sliding her hands out from under his to delve into her bag. "By the way, I got you a going away present."

Biting on the inside of her cheek to stop from laughing, she handed him the small black foil wrapped parcel. He turned it over several times, prodded and shook it, before slowly pulling on the gold ribbon binding it.

"Hurry up," she said. "We'll be in Rio by the time you open it."

"Haven't you heard the old saying good things come to those who wait..."

The rest of what he'd been about to say died on his lips as the wrapping fell open to reveal a matching pair of exquisite amethyst silk scarves he picked up and slid through his fingers, the slow, sensuous movement causing heat to flow through her body as he stared at her with desire.

"Does this mean you want to tie me up?"

"Forever," she murmured, tugging on the scarves, bringing him close enough to kiss.

"Sounds like a plan."

And as the plane taxied down the runway, they made a few more.

"Six months on the road at digs, six months in Melbourne for you to sculpt?" He asked.

"Deal."

"We keep the gallery and use it to showcase our talents?"

"Deal."

"We give this relationship a trial before doing the until death do us part thing?"

"No deal." Hating the momentary panic flaring on his face, she said, "Who needs a trial? Some smart guy once said we're both alike, being spontaneous and all. So how about it? You in this for the long haul?"

The tender glint in his eyes made her heart sing. "With you by my side, I'm up for anything."

"Really?" She sent a pointed glance at his groin, raising an eyebrow.

"You're killing me, Fancy Feet."

"Not yet, but it's a long flight, Professor," she said,

draping a blanket over his lap and sliding her hand up his thigh.

He clamped a hand over hers, laughing when she struggled and the blanket became a tug-o-war.

"I can get used to this." He angled in for a swift kiss that disarmed her completely. "Travelling together, having <u>fun</u> together..."

"I'm all for fun." She tugged the blanket back over the both of them and snuggled into him, more content than she'd ever been. "And I'm also all yours."

"Right back at you."

And as Aidan hugged her close, the plane soared skyward, and Beth hummed a corny ballad under her breath, she knew without a shadow of a doubt that some risks were worth taking.

All the way.

Ready to read Lana's story?
THE CEO.

All aboard...

When museum curator Lana takes a well-earned vacation on a cruise ship, the last thing she expects is to work. But Lana's always been a do-gooder and it's hard to break the habits of a lifetime, even when her brash cousin Beth insists she has a makeover before her trip.

Lana is a grumpy geek and proud of it. Until she meets fellow employee Zac, who's determined to tease her into playing...with him.

Zac has a secret and it's a doozy. With his company on the brink of collapse, he's determined to discover why, so going undercover on one of his cruise ships seems a sound plan for the CEO. But he doesn't count on being captivated by shy Lana and soon they're indulging in a steamy fling.

They're opposites in every way and once the ship docks, they'll go their separate ways.
Or will they?

READ IT NOW!

Read Nicola's newest feel-good romance <u>DID NOT FINISH</u>.
He's a bestselling author. She's a career-wrecking book reviewer.
Who will lose the plot first?

Or her new gothic, THE RETREAT.

Have you read the Bashful Brides series?

NOT THE MARRYING KIND

Who said marriage had to be convenient?
LA party planner Poppy's side business—planning divorce parties as the Divorce Diva—is a secret.
When a new party prospect gives Poppy the opportunity to save her sister's company, she can't pass it up.
But this time, she's about to get way more than she bargained for.

Vegas golden boy Beck knows Poppy's secret, and he's not afraid to use it to get exactly what he wants—a wife.
With his reputation on the line, the only way he can repair the damage is by getting hitched, fast.
And if blackmail is the only way to get Poppy to the altar, so be it.

But they're in the city of high stakes, and Poppy has a few aces up her sleeve.
It's time to find out if they're playing to win...or playing for keeps.

NOT THE ROMANTIC KIND

I'm a marine scientist. He's a CEO property developer out to ruin my family's coastal legacy. He's about to discover how far I'll go to protect what's mine.

Gemma loves her job, protecting the oceans from corporate sharks like Rory. So when the uptight property developer sets his sights on her family's beachside land, what's a woman to do but chain herself to his desk?

Rory hasn't got time for disruptions. He has a lot to prove and that means making Devlin Corp number one in the country. But maybe hiring the beautiful crusader Gemma can help his business? After all, what better way to prove his company is environmentally conscious than having her on staff?

Neither count on their unexpected attraction being stronger than the tides...

NOT THE DARING KIND

***I'm an architect. He's an incognito desert prince. He offers me the job of a lifetime, on one condition. I marry him.
As if.***

Bria thinks she's at the pinnacle of her career when she's invited to be a guest speaker at an architectural conference. She hasn't got time for Sam, a handsome distraction who woos her with romantic picnics and sizzling kisses. And when she leaves him behind and travels to the tiny desert municipality of Adhara, she's focussed one hundred percent on business.

*But Sam turns out to be the prince of Adhara and he offers her a dream job, to design an entire capital city. Bria can't refuse, not when her success to date has been tainted by her tyrannical father. But marrying the prince so he can ascend the throne is madness.
Isn't it?*

NOT THE DATING KIND

Fake dating her brother's best friend...

*If Eve has to attend another wedding without a date, she'll smash the cake with the bouquet she inevitably catches. So to avoid yet another well meaning fix-up from her besties, she reaches out to Bryce, her brother's best friend.
He's the perfect fake date candidate: gorgeous, successful, and in no danger of falling for her. He made that clear eight years ago when he rejected her the night of her brother's twenty-first.*

THE BOSS

Bryce is new to town and will do anything to impress his boss: including date Eve in exchange for her impressive business contacts. Eve's morphed from geek to chic but she's off-limits.

However, when lines are crossed and fake becomes real, will she stick around when he reveals his secret?

FREE BOOK AND MORE

SIGN UP TO NICOLA'S NEWSLETTER for a free book!

Read Nicola's newest feel-good romance **DID NOT FINISH**

Or her new gothic **THE RETREAT**

Try the **BASHFUL BRIDES** series

NOT THE MARRYING KIND

NOT THE ROMANTIC KIND

NOT THE DARING KIND

NOT THE DATING KIND

The **WORKPLACE LIAISONS** series

THE BOSS

THE CEO

The **CREATIVE IN LOVE** series

THE GRUMPY GUY

THE SHY GUY

THE GOOD GUY

Try the **BOMBSHELLS** series

BEFORE (FREE!)

BRASH

BLUSH

BOLD

BAD

BOMBSHELLS BOXED SET

The **WORLD APART** series

WALKING THE LINE (FREE!)

CROSSING THE LINE

TOWING THE LINE

BLURRING THE LINE

WORLD APART BOXED SET

The **HOT ISLAND NIGHTS** duo

WICKED NIGHTS

WANTON NIGHTS

The **BOLLYWOOD BILLIONAIRES** series

FAKING IT

MAKING IT

The **LOOKING FOR LOVE** series

LUCKY LOVE

CRAZY LOVE

SAPPHIRES ARE A GUY'S BEST FRIEND

THE SECOND CHANCE GUY

Check out Nicola's website for a full list of her books.

And read her other romances as Nikki North.

'MILLIONAIRE IN THE CITY' series.

LUCKY

COCKY

CRAZY

FANCY

FLIRTY

FOLLY

MADLY

Check out the **ESCAPE WITH ME** series.

DATE ME

LOVE ME

DARE ME

TRUST ME

FORGIVE ME

Try the **LAW BREAKER** series

THE DEAL MAKER

THE CONTRACT BREAKER

ABOUT THE AUTHOR

USA TODAY bestselling and multi-award winning author Nicola Marsh writes page-turning fiction to keep you up all night.

She's published 80 books and sold 8 million copies worldwide.

She currently writes contemporary romance and domestic suspense.

She's also a Waldenbooks, Bookscan, Amazon, iBooks and Barnes & Noble bestseller, a RBY (Romantic Book of the Year) and National Readers' Choice Award winner, and a multi-finalist for a number of awards including the Romantic Times Reviewers' Choice Award, HOLT Medallion, Booksellers' Best, Golden Quill, Laurel Wreath, and More than Magic.

A physiotherapist for thirteen years, she now adores writing full time, raising her two dashing young heroes, sharing fine food with family and friends, and her favorite, curling up with a good book!

Printed in Great Britain
by Amazon